Madman's Return

Peter J. Michael

Madman's Return

ISBN-13: 978-0-6459562-0-7

Published by Peter J. Michael

ALL BOOKS BY THIS AUTHOR ARE:

THE GREAT WAR AGAINST TERRORISM

KILLING THE BOGEYMAN I & II

RUTHLESS

RELIGIOUS DEATH TRAP

THE GOD OF ELIMINATION

THE MURDEROUS MR. A

MADMAN'S RETURN

Contents

Part One (Page 1-42)

Part Two (Page 43-98)

Part Three (Page 99-148)

Madman's Return

MADMAN'S RETURN

PART ONE

To Robert Stewart,

(No date, no name or signature by the sender.)

I am going to write this short story in a poetry format.
I hope you like poetry-style books, Robert Stewart.
Because the author of this story likes poetry-style books with an action-packed detective/crime twist.
You see, poetry format books helps me to cut through the bullshit and stick to the meat of the story.

So – to all, the whole world – and Robert Stewart – **ENJOY!**

I write this letter to you anonymously to tell you that you have a secret enemy out there in this world who hates you very much.
He wants sweet revenge against you for all the wrongs he says you have done to him.
He wants to hurt you very badly.
Then he plans to kill you.
But before he kills you, he wants to spar wits against you.

He is an expert gamesman-you are an expert gamesman.

First, he will spar with you, then he will destroy you.

Can you guess who I am writing about?

The secret enemy is very angry at you, Robert Stewart!
He wanted me to write this letter to you, so that he can test your smarts and see if you can figure out his identity.

Because if you can, it will be the shock of your life.

The secret enemy truly wants to shock you!
He wants to hurt you!

He wants to humiliate you and completely destroy your reputation – then kill you by putting you into the grave in complete shame - as he accused you of shaming him and costing him everything.

Again: do you know who I am writing about Robert Stewart?

He is planning a killing spree!
To destroy governors, mayors, the police, the politicians, the judges, the president – everyone whom he blames as responsible for his bitter fate!

The secret enemy plans to get revenge against everyone in society in order to hurt you, Robert Stewart!

He wants to in his own words: fuck you over!

He will destroy all those around you, including your family – and then he will destroy you completely before he kills you.

Have you figured out the identity of this person, Robert Stewart?

Take a guess!

You are a policeman with many enemies.
But only one has the power, the resources and the means to cause you irreparable harm – to those around you and especially to you-yourself!

Please Robert, don't sweat too much in fear of the unknown.
The enemy does not want you dead – YET!

The enemy wants you to sweat it out first in unimaginable fear before he comes after you with his final deathblow!

Do you know who I am talking/writing about, Robert Stewart?

The secret enemy really wants you to figure out his secret identity, but he will not make it too easy for you.
You will have to work your brain to unravel the true mysteries of your life.

As I wrote before: the secret enemy plans to utterly destroy you completely.
And then he will kill all those around you, including your family – and then he will finish with engraving his own signature on your

tombstone – as the man responsible for putting you in the grave!

Robert Stewart: you are a hero in this town.
You have solved many cases before this one.
But the secret enemy guarantees you will never solve this case!

He is bigger than the world.
He is bigger than life.
He is bigger than you, Robert Stewart!

Soon the murders will start.

And you policeman, will take pictures of all the murders.
You will pin them on the police wall of your evidence board.
But you will never be able to solve the crimes!

The murders will be done in similar MO with a cultish twist!

But the murders will remain forever unsolved.
And the secret enemy will remain forever unapprehended.

You can ransack every house and hideout in New York City – but you will never find this secret enemy.

He will find you, but you can never see him!

Perhaps the secret enemy will implicate you in many of the mass murders.

He will drive you crazy and then people will think you're a crazy cop who began to kill people out of spite!

Can you sense the bad storm heading to New York City?

And you Robert Stewart are going to be right in the middle of it.

You will have no solid alibi and credible witnesses to account for your whereabouts when the murders begin.

Even your police buddies will hunt you down in order to stop you – to kill you.

The police and your secret enemy will both be coming after you.
You will have nowhere to run, Robert Stewart.

And the killings will go on and on until you crack!

The enemy wants to drive you to complete madness as the world has accused him of madness – you too will be condemned to the very same madness.
You will become a killer cop on the run and your own police friends will hunt you down when they see how much evidence there is against you.

It will be a staggering amount of evidence!

It will not be circumstantial.

There will be eyewitness accounts to your sordid crimes.
And the police will hunt for your blood.
Because where bad cops are concerned, all cops believe that they deserve the worst!

The SECRET ENEMY was crying blood in the grave for what you did to him, Robert Stewart!
And he wants to pay you back for all the horrible things he has accused you of doing to him!

Your actions in the past against him, have driven your enemy to insane depths of madness!

Hell is coming to New York Robert Stewart!

Your secret enemy is going to kill masses of people in order to get back at you for everything you have done to him!

After your bitter enemy is finished with you, even your own police friends will want you dead!
They will want to hang you.
They will want to shoot you on sight!
How could you blame them?

Because the secret enemy knows you well, Robert Stewart!
He knows that you would do the same thing if you were in their position.

It will be bad!
Your predicament will be very bad!

Even solitary confinement with 24-hour guards around you will not be able to protect you from the hell that is headed your way, good copper!

8

The secret enemy will make everyone want you dead.

The mob, the police, society – everyone.

And you cannot run away.
Because you will not be able to count on anyone.
Everyone you know will turn against you.
Everyone will want to kill you, Robert Stewart!

Be ready Robert Stewart: because soon, you will be sent to hell.
And your true enemy will torment you there!
He will make you cry blood.
He wants to hear you scream.

I think you should get the advice of a good bookie.
And place a bet – to wager who is going to win this game.
You or your enemy?
But don't worry, it will be a fair fight.
He will first cut you in pieces before he crucifies what is left of you.

No cop takes kindly when one of their own turns bad.

And that is exactly what the secret enemy will
do to you.
He will destroy your reputation as you have
destroyed his.

The district attorney and the police
commissioner of your precinct will order you to
be shot on sight, even before you are put on
trial.
That will be the order of your enemy!

The secret enemy will arrange for all your other
enemies to line up against you – those in prison
and those yet roaming the streets.

The world will become a very ugly place for
you, Robert Stewart!

Get ready: peace will become war.

Many people will die and so will you.

The secret enemy believes that you deserve the
worst Robert Stewart for what you did to him.
And he plans to get even.
He wants to waste you!

You are a strong independent man whom no
one can influence.

But your enemy will push you over, Robert
Stewart!
Your enemy is stronger and smarter than you,
Robert Stewart.

If I too did not hate you, I would pity what is
about to happen to you!

I will give you a clue as to my identity.
I am your secret enemy's doctor-his surgeon.
He told me to send you this letter as he dictated
the crux of its contents to me.

There is no escape for you anymore from your
enemy's wrath!
You will become up to your neck in the shit he
is about to throw your way.

So don't alert the Highway Patrol!
Because they will not be able to find this Secret
Enemy.

Forget the police helicopters, the dogs and the
reinforcements – it will be useless against your
enemy!

The entire fucking United States Marine Corps
couldn't catch him!
Nor outfight him!

The only thing left for you to do Robert Stewart is to sit down and eat your fingernails to the bone.

You are helpless.
And the world is hopeless against the secret enemy!
Your enemy will beat you at your own police game, Robert Stewart!
And his victory will be sweet!

Don't bother wiretapping every home and every phone installation of every resident in the city – because you will never pinpoint the enemy's location.
You will never be able to flush him out!
But he is watching your every move Robert Stewart!
He knows what you will do even before you do it.
He can even read your mind.
As you have thousands of pages of secret dossiers of your targets, the enemy as well, is brilliant in his cunning ways!

And if truth be told: you are no match for him, Robert Stewart!
You will never beat him!

You can order New York City to be locked up
tighter than a drum with no one allowed to
enter or exit its borders.
But you will still never find him.

Robert Stewart: your luck has run out!

No one can save you!

And you cannot even save yourself!

What is your belief system, Robert Stewart?
Is it: the law is the law!

Well, your enemy is now the new law!
And your time has just run out!

You are mortal!
Your enemy is omnipotent!

Watch where you walk, Robert Stewart.
The enemy may order a heavy crate to come
crashing down on your head.
Perhaps a gunman or gunmen might be ordered
to tail you and shoot you in the street!

Be afraid, Robert Stewart!
Be plenty fearful.
Your world is coming to an end.

Your life is hanging in the balance.
Tick-tock, tick-tock, tick-tock, tick-tock...
Perhaps he might plant a bomb inside your
house and your car.

Don't be too paranoid Robert Stewart.
Your enemy is a master gamesman.
And this game between you and him has only
just begun.

Watch your step Robert Stewart: a vicious gang
is being sent to destroy you, good copper - and
the entire citizens of New York City will be
intentionally caught in the crossfire!
Can you hear the screams of every man, woman
and child in the entire state of New York?
It will be hell unleashed!

Robert Stewart: I strongly suggest you never
leave the protection of your police station - and
I urge you to work fervently on your list of
suspects to pin on your evidence board.
See who the enemy is.
Hopefully your list of suspects aren't longshots.
Can you pinpoint the real identity of the culprit
who has a true motive of hatred against you?
Can you determine the connection between you
and him, Master Detective Robert Stewart?

Because the enemy is nothing but bad news for you and the entire city and state of New York. All of you are going to shake at his rage directed your way!

But I will give you a clue as to who he is.

He is extremely powerful, influential and wealthy enough to buyout the entire city of New York and everybody in it.

Your enemy at this point knows what you are thinking Robert Stewart.
He knows your mind is conjuring wild thoughts at this point to put him out of commission.
Perhaps you might want to send him to Siberia!
Forget it, Robert Stewart!
You could not even find him.
He is concealed that cleverly.
You will never find him.
You will never be able to get anywhere near him.
But, at the same time, he will be able to watch your every movement and with a click of a finger, he can order your death at any moment!
And any place!

So, start hauling in your list of suspects one by one into your police office.

Start questioning which one of them hates you enough to want to squeeze the very guts out of you, without a second thought to spilling the blood of every single citizen in New York, in order to punish and hurt you severely, Robert Stewart!

Maybe by now you have one suspect in mind.
Perhaps you have a hundred.
And perhaps you have one question for each of them or many questions to ask them.

But no matter what, your true enemy assures you, you will never receive the answers you seek, unless of course he wants you to know and leads you directly to the correct conclusion!

How is the list of suspects on your police station evidence board going?
Is it beginning to tear out your guts?

Figuring out the identity of the enemy who wants to hurt you so badly will be such an enormous feat for you to solve, police copper Robert Stewart!

Can you feel your enemy slipping away from your overzealous clutches?

You have a big problem on your hands as you are out on the street working on this case. And the problem is: that you will never be able to solve it.

I am sure by now you are busting your butt trying to solve this case and apprehend the enemy, that is if you can figure out his identity on time to stop him from unleashing the bloodbath in the city, in which he is planning to get back at you with!

But don't fret too much Robert Stewart at the prospect that you will never guess who he is, nor will you be able to stop him on time from killing and committing mass murder against the townsfolk of New York City, in order to get back at you!
Your enemy is the new big shot omerta boss in town who plans to take over business after business, until he completely runs New York City and every corporation in it, whilst at the same time eliminating his competition and all those allies of yours, copper Robert!

I am sure by now Robert, you are sweating it out, shouting to your police colleagues inside your police station office saying: 'Damn I would love to get the goods on this guy and stop him cold!'

But it is useless.

The enemy controls everything, including manufacturing computers.
So, if he wants to send you an anonymous message by computer to your police computer, you will never be able to trace him.
Because he is an expert at anonymity!

I am sure by now Robert Stewart that this case is getting to you.
And in your mind, in your heart and your very soul, you are begging for it not to be able to continue.
But it will continue Robert Stewart!
In fact, the **game** has only just begun!

Robert Stewart – you can run on foot, you can drive in one vehicle, dump it and use another vehicle to attempt to elude your trailers, but the enemy will always track you down.
Your whereabouts will never be a secret from him!

You can hide in a cave or you can blend in a crowd, but you will never remain invisible from your number one true enemy!

Robert Stewart: we all know you are a highly-trained professional cop.
You are very crafty, clever and cunning.
But always remember: the enemy is more crafty, clever and cunning than you.
He will always be one step ahead of you!
He is more of an enemy to you than you are to him: one of the utmost and extreme deadliest proportions!

The enemy will begin drying up all the monetary fortunes out of all foreign and domestic bank accounts of all his competitors.
He will have inside contacts in all banks and access to everyone's account numbers and passwords.
He will strip the world of their fortunes and takeover everything they own, and he will destroy the world – and he will destroy you, Robert Stewart!
He will give you prank phone calls and stir up strife after strife after strife in your chicken hearts.
For all of you!

You can bug all residents' houses in New York.
You can tap their phone calls.
You can hunt for every secret room above
ground or beneath the floors of all houses in
your city, but you will still never locate your
number one enemy.
He is smarter and cleverer than you Robert.
He is even tougher than you.
So, watch out.
Be on guard.
He is coming for you.
He wants revenge against you Robert Stewart!

It doesn't matter Robert if you are an expert at
disguises.
You can even be disguised as the country
President's 110-year-old grandmother.
We will still find you.
And you Robert, with your police dragnet and
all your roadblocks covering every major
highway and side street in New York City, will
still never find the **secret enemy!**

So, study your evidence board, coordinate
police procedures out in the field from your
station house office and in the street, with your
armies of police and government men.
The hunt for your enemy will be in vain!
Completely fruitless.

You will never catch him!

You can have the entire city of New York swarming with cops hunting for the enemy and trying to kill him.
But you will fail.
Your dragnet to lock the entire state tighter than a drum will not succeed against your number one target.
All your roadblocks and SWAT teams on alert – and even in addition with the United States Marine Corps, will surely be fruitless.
It will amount to zero!

Robert Stewart: you have already lost the battle and the war itself.
Accept your fate.
Accept your destiny.
You are the enemy's target, not the other way around.
Vengeance will be his.
He will have his revenge against you and not you nor your people will be able to stop it!
You will never find him and you will never stop him from killing all you people!

How is your brain feeling?
Have you tapped into that deductive reasoning to figure out what you need to know: the

identity of the man who hates you more than anything in this world?

Your enemy sees your guns and hears the swarms of police cars and their blazing sirens roaring across every street and highway in the city out looking for him.

But you know his reaction against you and your police efforts against him?
He just laughs at your failed attempts to find him.
You can hunt and chase but you will lose and he will win!
Why?
Because you are really chasing a ghost.
You don't know who he is.
He is brilliant and cunning.
He is a genius as always.
You are no match for him Robert Stewart.
But he thanks you for entertaining him as you attempt to go after him, the worthy opponent he always considers you to be.
And good luck in the hunt: the game of cat and mouse.
The enemy is the cat and you as always are the mouse, Robert Stewart!

The enemy is smiling at your news bulletin broadcasted on all television networks and every radio station all across the country by anxious reporters to the public, which states: **In New York this day, the police are still in hunt for suspected mass murderer 'The Ghost' – who is still at large making threats on everyone's lives, especially his arch-enemy Robert Stewart.**

The police have set up roadblocks across the entire state of New York and put in place effective immediately a citywide dragnet, in order to apprehend their invisible and dangerous target!

Robert Stewart has ordered the heavy artillery and armies of police out searching for his anonymous enemy, who is threatening not only his life, but the lives of every man, woman and child which resides in New York City!

The police have ordered to shoot their target on sight with the latest shoot-to-kill order being authorized by all the local police chief commissioners in unanimous decision across the entire vicinity of New York State.

You see Robert, the enemy knows your every movement even before you make them.

He knows what you will do and are doing as we speak, so to speak.

He knows you and your police colleagues do not mess around.

You have authorized the execution of a man you don't even know the identity of.

'The Ghost' – is that not what you will label him?

Good luck Robert in your endeavours to find him.

Because you never will!

Even if he tells you who he is – you still will never find him.

That is how invisible he has made himself to not only you, but to the entire world at large.

Let me explain everything to you.

Your enemy has authorized me to NOW give you the biggest piece of the puzzle you need, so that **the ghost** you are chasing no longer remains a ghost!

He will now give you the biggest piece of the puzzle you need, the greatest clue, to hopefully unravel the great mystery of all mysteries to his true identity.

Are you ready for the real challenge Robert Stewart, to solve the case of this mysterious target of yours?
And then, the real challenge will be to catch him if you can and stop him from killing everyone in New York, including your family.
And then – then finally his lengthy plans of revenge he, in his own words, describes as: eliminating you, Robert Stewart!

The enemy will first lead you to his true identity and then he will drive you and your police colleagues' crazy trying to find him, in order to save your tails as marked men!

So happy hunting Robert Stewart!
Because you are truly looking and searching for 'The Ghost of Christmas Past!'
So, try to find him!
Try to kill him!
Because if you don't, you are all dead men!
He will surely kill you all!

'The Enemy' has been planning his revenge against you for a very long time.
He put in place all the intricate details for his **master plan** of revenge against the world and you Robert Stewart!

And he waited until he planned everything perfectly to the most minute detail, before he would resurface and cast his great revenge against all - the whole world - and you Robert Stewart, in a practical measure.

CAN YOU NOW GUESS WHO HE IS?

Here are the clues to his master plan.
This is what he had achieved and planned, plotted and put in place.

You see, the secret enemy was a certified dead man.
And he surely did not want to leave the world in vain with his enemies getting the upper hand.
So, he planned quite brilliantly to make a comeback after his otherwise demise, if you will.

Him and I (his doctor and surgeon), had very secret meetings together, only the two of us.
We figured a way that his legacy of hate and vengeance may live on once his old form had expired from the world.
This is what we came up with…
So read the untraceable computer printout notes very carefully Robert - and figure out the

missing pieces to the puzzle – because it is what the secret enemy wants.

This was and is the Master Plan of the Secret Enemy: Robert Stewart: I will give you another clue to your worst adversary's identity.
First, he was ashes, now he is no longer ashes!
Did he have his body cremated?
Forget the preliminary report.
Check the full conclusive coroner's report into his death!
And get a court order to exhume the body from its grave.
And investigate everything thoroughly.
See if anything is missing?
Any vital organs taken out of his body?
Anything removed whatsoever?
They have tests.
They have dental records.
They can perform very many extensive tests.
They have the size, shape and weight of bones.
They can even recreate the damaged head-kicked face from the skull of a severed head.
All the answers are in front of you Robert Stewart.

Forensic medicine is a fascinating and complicated part of pathology.

Sometimes results can and cannot be forthcoming, depending on what remains are found to identify.

Missing heads, bodies and hearts make it tricky for your lab boys to determine heads or tails to answers you need right now Robert Stewart.

But you are credited as being a clever and resourceful policeman.

You should be able to make a clear determination of the facts.

The coroner's report into his death should make fascinating news.

Just as the secret enemy I choose to call, **'The Deathless Great Master'** – has influence with all banks' presidents across the world, to steal people's so-called secure money and hidden fortunes, even the coroner is at his disposal, to falsify reports and tamper with evidence for a price.

And **'The Deathless Great Master'** can blackmail and threaten any journalist to write any story and make in his own words: **'the world of fools and imbeciles believe it!'**

Robert Stewart: you are headed for war with the devil himself!

Your opponent is endless, indestructible, enduring, undying and deadly.

He is never-ending.
He is timeless and eternal.
He is all-knowing and all-seeing, boundless and infinite.

Isn't it ironical?
He was actually dead and now…now he lives on!
That is a true glowing testament to the great infinite powers of - **The Deathless Great Master!**

This is how he did it…
These are the plans we discussed in private just the two of us, prior his physical death years ago, so that his legacy of revenge and hate could live on and on and on – **FOREVER!**
Yes, forever uninterrupted!

We both decided on the perfect plan to have his legacy live on and continue eternally against the world.
And that was for the dying enemy to donate his healthy and strong heart to a suitable recipient, who came close to matching his great powerful enigmatic appearance as the donor had truly resembled in his prime.

So, when the heart of a powerful figure as your enemy becomes transplanted into another strong figure of a man - hence the great master plan takes effect: the role of cellular memory: personality changes following heart transplantation.

And that means as has been reported for decades, whereby the recipient acquired the personality characteristics of the donor.

The entire recipient's personality had altered. His personal preferences changed to the donor's.

His transference of identity, emotions, temperament and complete memories from the donor's life now entered the heart recipient's being.

The heart recipient became an exact replica of the donor's hostile and maniacal personality.

The recipient liked what the donor liked.

And the recipient hated what the donor hated: meaning, in his own words: the world of wimps, weaklings, lying cunts and fucking jealous scumbags!

Following the heart organ transplant, it became a classic case of memory transference from the donor to the recipient.

The recipient now has inherited the memory, emotions, likes, dislikes and personal and professional experiences of the donor.

The drastic personality change of the recipient was remarkable.

The recipient was now the donor.

The mind and body began communicating perfectly through chemicals known as peptides, found in muscles and major organs such as the brain, stomach and heart.

So, the dead and dying enemy would live on his old form and character traits in another being as I had predicted, following the successful heart transplant surgery.

And thus, the memory could be accessed throughout the peptide/receptor network.

For instance, feelings of love and hate could be accessed from the heart and transplanted from one person to another!

The heart is one organ which contains a network of neurotransmitters that can be seen as a second brain.

The heart organ is very intelligent.

The heart can often lead the brain both in interpretations of external worldly factors and its people - and lead the actions individuals choose to take, whether for good or bad, the benefit or destruction of others!

I lived to see and witness the true miracle of heart transplant and cell memory phenomenon,

in terms of personality changes of the recipient matching the donor.
Now the recipient and donor were quite similar in their quirks and desires.

The recipient's personality had changed to match his donor's.

And in the enemy's case, those quirks and desires were complete hatred and unending wishful longing for volcanic retribution!

So, when the enemy was dead and done with into the grave, he died still knowing that it would not be totally in vain, via the donation of his heart to a suitable candidate, who would henceforth inherit his feelings of love and hate - and continue his firm desire for vendettas against the entire world of what he described as: loathsome people!

****

Robert Stewart had the police lab check the report letter for fingerprints and any possible DNA, but none were found.
And there was nothing uncommon with the paper or printer the letter was typed on.
If the paper and/or print was unique, they could narrow down the search questioning possible print shop owners and employees for a small list of purchasers' names.

Robert almost felt gravely ill at the sudden discovery he made, as he uncovered the secret identity of his vicious enemy, though feared to speak the name of the target at first.
But he eventually did.
In himself, only one person could be sick enough to be behind these evil words, evil conspiracies and otherwise evil actions:
Domenico Armando!

Robert was bothered with numerous questions into the deadly ordeal he now faced.
He began thinking logical questions to himself concerning this very illogical dilemma he was now entangled within.
He knew his enemy's identity.
But he did not have any concrete knowledge or solid evidence as to his reported heart transplant (recipient's) new identity.

Domenico was still out there again.

But who is he now?
Who took his heart?
And was it consensual?

Did the heart transplant recipient really know
the true identity of his donor?

Was it part of Domenico's plan before his
death, to trick someone into having his heart
implanted into his body, to replace the
recipient's sick heart, so that he could inherit
Domenico's sick and twisted personality and
character traits, in order to continue
Domenico's insane lunacy and deranged
vindictiveness inside another body – especially
against me – Robert Stewart?
And the bigger question was, who is Domenico
now?

Is he the mayor?
Is he the governor?
Is he the Archbishop of New York?

He could be anyone who had a heart transplant
in recent times!
I have to figure out a way to trace all the top-
secret steps leading to that heart transplant

recipient – and figure out who exactly took the enemy's heart – so I can get to that man first – now transformed into a maniac Domenico once was when he was alive.
And I have to stop this bastard cold in his tracks, or else a great many lives will be destroyed, even killed if I do not find this sick man in time.
Because if he is not captured and destroyed, then Domenico's would-be reincarnation inside another body will spell absolute hell for the world – and the complete destruction of everyone who resides inside it.
And that can never be allowed to happen.

Domenico is just as chaotic as Hitler, and even in many ways – that bastard Armando is a whole hell of a lot worse!
Because Domenico is deadly to everyone and everything that walks the face of the earth, in more grave proportions than any other dictator before him.
I have to find him first before he kills a great many more people!

****

Robert Stewart would begin his investigation immediately into the identity of Domenico Armando's secret surgeon doctor.

Who was he?

What was his name?

All in all, Robert would possibly be able to track him via secret payoffs made in secret front dummy banks accounts (either locally or interstate and overseas), he may have received from Domenico before and after Armando's death, in order to remove his heart from his corpse as the evil donor to some mysterious heart transplant recipient.

Whoever that man was!

There were a lot of unanswered questions right now.

And Robert was determined to find out all of the answers and soon, before this newly-reincarnated Domenico Armando begins his diabolically insane killing spree across New York City – to begin with!

Robert Stewart was up against a very dark and sinister conspiracy – and he had to psyche himself to complete readiness for the great challenge that lay ahead of him.

In the meantime, Robert Stewart planned to be extremely extra careful from this point on.
He had to take very many safety precautions to ensure the enemy did not snoop in on his intricate plans to smoke him out.

Robert had to make sure the opponent did not plant secret hidden surveillance equipment inside his house and/or his car.
No cameras and no microphones.
So, Robert had to be on guard and check everywhere inside his private properties before he discussed his secret plans himself against the enemy with his police partner John McCallum and his brother Paul.
Robert had to make sure that he was not being watched by the opponent as he planned to find him.
The **game plan** had to also include top secrecy on his part.
The enemy could not know any of his movements against him.
So, Robert had to safeguard against any possible 'secret surveillance system' the adversary may plant around him.

Robert was familiar with electronic surveillance and no matter what state-of-the-art systems the enemy would throw his way, Robert planned to foil the enemy's hopes of getting any ideas of being one step ahead of him in the 'game' or the 'new game' they currently faced.

The deadly lethal game it surely was! Robert understood perfectly that he had to be extra careful not to expose himself and his plans prematurely to their invisible foe, who surely controlled his invisible army both from a long and short distance away, the master criminal Domenico always was!

Henceforth, if Robert found the possible planted surveillance equipment, he would plan to trace it back to the manufacturer, who sold it, and also who designed it and who made it (without tipping off the enemy or his people) - as a possible lead to Domenico's people, they could use to trace the mastermind antagonist's whereabouts.

And if Robert found he was bugged, he would firstly not mention anything important the opponent could use effectively against him around such areas and rooms under surveillance and secondly, he would only say things in order to trick and set up the enemy, to lure him out of hiding for a supposed face-to-face meeting.

Robert would lie to the antagonist via his possible surveillance plants concealed around him if necessary.

So, Robert would make sure the room he discussed his true plans against the enemy was clean and unmonitored.

Robert would quickly get his hands on electronic detectors to sweep his house and car both thoroughly and discreetly, to see exactly what they were up against – and ascertain what movements their invisible enemy and his invisible armies were exactly plotting against him.

And no matter how well-concealed the surveillance traps were – Robert planned to search his properties carefully for them and find every single eavesdropping device thrown against him, as well as the hidden receivers to pick up his secret conversations - for purposes of attack against the enemy.

And to find the location of where such possible surveillance equipment would be operated from, via tracing the receiver, especially by obtaining a search warrant from a convinced judge into any possible suspect's house or suspects.

Besides, that highly incriminating letter by the enemy and his doctor which was sent to his police station house office, would make obtaining a search warrant, mere child's play!

Anyhow, tracing the address to the rightful owner of possible planted surveillance devices was necessary, which could surely prove as a positive lead to the mastermind's whereabouts or his people and cronies who could lead them to him.

****

Robert Stewart had now prepared himself for what was coming for him.

Robert Stewart planned to head to the streets immediately and get some action going in his crusade against the enemy, to hunt down his hidden location.

And he also armed himself with various elaborate disguises to remain invisible himself, so the evil opponent could not track his movements against him if he could not spot him.

And Robert would mostly (not always), but mostly be working the streets in the **cover of darkness!**

The key was to move in silence!

Even before his death, Robert Stewart knew that Domenico Armando was seeking revenge against his enemies – and for that revenge to continue after his death – even within the walls of his coffin!

Domenico Armando planned many years ago to haunt everyone from even the grave. From his grave, he intended that no one would ever be rid of him and free from his brutally vengeful wrath!

The bitter enemy wanted to destroy everyone
even after his death.
And it seemed as though, his horrible
destructive plans for revenge had succeeded.

Robert Stewart also knew that **'hell'** was
headed for New York City.
And he psyched his mind and his heart and his
soul to absolute readiness, for all-out war
between him and his evil opponent to begin at
any time NOW!

PART TWO

The ferocious Boss Man called **'The CZAR'** by his private army, had assembled his mass targets of despicable men and despicable women, inside his secret dungeon to be tortured to death!

The man known as the CZAR (as he was referenced, because of his superior stature as an autocratic ruler and leader of leaders-a person exercising great power and great authority over all others), ordered his armed hitmen soldier people to exact **justice** against his labelled 'scum' targets, by being brutally ruthless and extremely evil towards them!

The Czar had haunting recollections of his previous life before completely dying and being beheaded, as he was sent to a dark grim horrible place of hellfire!

The Boss Man was not placed inside the general population section of his hellish eternal reality, but instead, he was locked up inside one of the dungeon rooms of the very special sections of pits and caves, designed for special cases of evil as himself.

He was lying completely naked on his back (the condition of nudity only adding further to his absolute state of vulnerability), with his arms forced apart behind him, his wrists bolted by shackles onto the hot concrete ground – and his legs also spread apart – as his ankles were bolted the same way with shackles, so he could not move at all.

Then he was placed alone inside his terrible dungeon quarters, unable to breathe.

(Because inside hell, the cool oxygen situated outside the dark tunnel of the gates of hellfire, was replaced by this extremely hot, heavy and suffocating toxicity, that caused all the trapped damned souls confined, not only to experience suffocation for all eternity, as one of the many torments they endured, but also, the hot and heavy toxicity replacing the oxygen outside the gates of hell, felt extremely heavy as a mountain, forcing the damned souls to also become paralysed, unable to move and breathe as demons and fire tortured them.)

But inside his special cavern, as he was bolted onto the concrete ground, unable to breathe, move or defend himself, he witnessed a huge and massively grotesque, extremely sewer smelly, evil and sadistic angry ugly demon enter his dungeon, holding a great big sharp sword with one of his gruesome black, hairy sharp-clawed hands, he then raised with both clawed hands above his frightening monstrous-looking head, and sent it down on him hard at lightning speed.

The sharp heavy blade attacking him everywhere – and including his ribs and tearing down to his crotch area, ripping him apart, first splitting his body in two, then severing him in pieces, flesh and bones.

The very huge demon kept cutting him up – and then satisfied his hunger by eating his flesh in front of him and chewing on his torn bones. (And keeping leftovers as reserves hanging on sharp spikes on top of the fencing surrounding the dungeon.)

So, the demon was used to torture him, by cutting him up, and satisfying his hunger by eating him alive.

And because inside the place of torment he was given a spirit flesh, the body would eventually grow back to its original state, so the same tortures of the anguished mind and mutilated body, would be inflicted upon him numerous times a day, every day and every night – forever and ever!

NOW, the Boss Man Czar, strengthened his mind to suffer his victims the same way in which he had suffered, as he assembled his targets neatly inside the great big dungeon room, situated inside his newly-purchased Brooklyn, New York mansion.

The dungeon was a secret room he had specifically designed to fix his enemies upon death, trapping them inside.

He had his army legion of armed soldiers strip down his targeted men and women, all 97 of them in total, completely naked.

And had his target victims fixed the same way onto the concrete floor – with arms and legs forced apart, their wrists and ankles bolted to the concrete floor, the same way he experienced in his other life in hell.

And his soldier people were each armed with a large Samurai sword grasped in both hands, ready to start the mass executions and death sentences by mutilations, butchery and torture of the Czar's labelled, 'scum' targets.

The Czar shouted to his now forced defenceless targets, a fiery condemnation filled with pure hatred and fury and rage, directed at them and their crimes against him: You killed a beautiful girl who I considered a true daughter as she considered me her real father.

She was an author, a very talented book writer of fiction.

And you male and female scums lined up onto the floor here were all brick-and-mortar bookstore owners, operatives and printing company owner, employees and managers, gathered from all sections of the country.

My sweet daughter published her first book last month.

It was a great novel.

She was a gifted writer.

A very talented artist.

I spent millions of dollars buying over a million copies of her novel from all across the country, to help her promote her book, in which you scums so happened to operate inside such businesses.

And you fucking rats played games with her.

Very sick and evil mind games.

Because you fuckwits were all jealous of her talents and her success and accomplishments - when you were all failures in comparison, accomplishing nothing but zero in your shit lives.

So, you all decided to join together, to come after my daughter out of greed and jealousy.

You all sought to attack and dishonour her callously and unconscionably, for NO reason.

Only because you all were miserably envious of what she had – and what you could never accomplish on your own!

You shits knew she was gifted – and of course, because you are all jealous losers, failures and cocksucker scums, who don't have the brains to accomplish anything more than stupidity and mediocrity in this world - to raise yourselves out of your shit inconsequential existences - you chose to play games with her, very sick games, diabolical mind games, to attempt to toy with her mind and destroy her confidence.

You paid your associates in your line of work to plot and scheme to give her book bad publicity so it does not sell.

You also gave her bad reviews.

You even tried to pay men to become friends with her, have sex with her in order to learn about her creative talents, to steal her ideas as well as her money from her.

You would all lie publicly that her book was bad, but privately, you were envious of her talents - and tried to steal her book, plagiarize her work and sell her innovative original ideas as your own.

You also paid your evil associate friends in the book printing and bookstore industry, to send my daughter bad letters, telling her she should not write.

That she was no good.
And should not pursue her dream of being a best-selling writer.
You also all plotted to steal her book sales, the millions of dollars in sales of her book I created for her.
You did that because you are greedy failures and zero IQ scumbags, every male and female cocksucker one of you.
Some of you bookstore operatives and owners had written novels yourselves.
But your novels were of shit quality.
So, you tried to bring my daughter down to appease your own failures in writing.
You jealous cocksuckers tried to compete with my brilliant daughter.
But you losers and failures, really cannot do anything of value or accomplish anything of substance, besides plotting lies cowardly behind everyone's backs, to bring people to your shit level of nothingness.
Huh.
You all tried to compete with my daughter and her great artistic skills.
But what you failed to realise, is that: **you cannot compete where you do not compare!**

And because of the games you played with my beautiful twenty-year-old daughter – and all the

money, the millions of dollars you stole from her, it broke her spirit, shattered her mind and destroyed her confidence.
And forever messed with her brain.

She slashed her wrists, opened up her veins and began bleeding to death, as she sat alone in front of her computer, inside her room within the walls of my mansion.
She killed herself before the computer that she used to write her great book with.
Because of all you scums, she killed herself.
You scum men and women I gathered here as sheep for the slaughter, murdered my daughter – and now I will kill you all one million-and millions of times worse, outmatching the agony you caused my sweet daughter when she decided to end her life – and also outmatching the money you stole from her-all those multimillions.

Before you all die, you want to know the true definition of stupid?
It is what you fucking scumbags look at every time you see yourselves in the mirror.
You cunts are the true definition of stupid!
Stupid is when you fuck with someone you know nothing about.

You idiots do not know what sort of an enemy I am.

You do not know what I am capable of-what I will do to each and every one of you.

Well, you are just about to find out, when I inflict upon you all a true hellish experience. And please scream at the top of your lungs. That will please me very much, as much as the slow-torturous deaths which I will also inflict upon you all this very moment!

The Czar relished watching the terrified expressions displayed on each of their faces, as they were bolted completely naked, onto the cold concrete floor, unable to move.

NOW, he would make them painfully regret ever fucking with his precious daughter, who died because of these filthy book printing and bookstore business owners, operatives and employees – and their detestably deceptive ways, and intentionally callous robbery and robberies of his beloved daughter's artistic monetary fortunes.

The Czar's cherished daughter, as he considered her, had self-published her work as opposed to traditional publishing, because she wanted complete control of her book.

She wanted it written her way, especially without any traditional publisher and editor ripping it apart and ruining her proud ideas. The Czar paid a lot of money to print copies of her novel, using the printing company in Brooklyn, New York, his daughter set up her book with - and stocking them in bookstores all over the country.

The printing company had its own retail sales division.

The Czar's daughter initially would set up her book nationally – and once it was established throughout the United States, the Czar had ambitions to promote her great work all over the world!

But her dream was cut short upon her death. Her dream was destroyed.

Her talent was unrecognised and killed off – the same way the Czar now planned to maim, kill and destroy all those responsible for putting the girl he described as 'my beloved daughter' into the grave.

Both bookstores and printer personnel stole all her money she earnt in sales – **and now the Czar was delivering his 'justice' against all of them!**

Moments before giving his henchmen the final go-ahead to do away with his targets, the Czar disclosed one final tidbit of information to these considered 'shitheads' gathered before him: I have taken the pleasure in liberating all your bank account numbers and banking details for the sole purpose, to take all the money back that you stole from my daughter.
And I have also taken the rest of your savings, now in my possession.
I have taken everything you own as payback – as surely as right now I will take your fucking miserable lives from each and every one of you!

The Boss Man Czar ordered his legion of soldiers armed with Samurai swords to get to work on his fucking scum targets – and mutilate them to death.
They cut off their hands, their feet, then their arms and legs.
And castrated the men and cut off the breasts of the women.
Then each of the killer soldiers were ordered to cut off their ears, their noses and cut out each of their eyes.
And using the soles of their steal-capped boots, the expert assassins were then commanded to raise their feet and send them crashing down

full force on their faces, smashing all their teeth.

Once it was decided by their master boss, that they had suffered complete and utter despair, much to his complete satisfaction, the Czar then demanded to finish them off by beheading all the male and female scum trash, who were all lined up against the other on the concrete floor of the dark dungeon, awaiting their bloody mutilations – then final death sentences to be unleashed, finally ending their long screams, which pleased immensely the emotions of the Boss Man.

For the screams of his male and female trashy targets fell upon his senses much like music to his ears.

As they were all tortured to death, the **CZAR** was satisfied that justice was finally executed against all those fucking cocksuckers responsible for killing his beautiful precious daughter!

The **CZAR** then ordered his people: Make the mutilated bodies of all these scums disappear without a trace.

And then clean this room perfectly!

His army of henchmen nodded their heads dutifully, obeying his every word and every order to perfection!

The Czar then rapidly adjourned to his private den inside his New York City mansion.
His mansion was situated on 16th Avenue in Brooklyn.
The Czar spoke to his considered son Marcus, the brother of his now deceased sister, Maria.

The bull-like, strong-built Czar who wore a black silk robe, then embraced his mild-featured and mild-mannered, lean-structured, dark-skinned and straight black-haired son in greeting inside his private office.
His son Marcus, whose hair was parted at one side, and dressed casually in jeans and a leather jacket, also considered the Czar a true father.
Marcus was pleased at his equally considered father's methods of justice delivered against the men and women responsible for his sister's death.
Although he was not present inside the death chamber when the massacres took place, he was glad to hear the news of their deaths at his father's hands and his father's will.

The Czar confided to his twenty-five-year-old Italian son Marcus all his secret plans for the not-so-distant future.

He insisted: My son Marcus: I have great plans of revenge and destruction against the scum, not only in this country of the United States, but the world at large for all its heinous sins!

You see, my great son Marcus, to the outside world I am Italian-born Maestro Dante Rolando.

A famous conductor.

I chose the perfect candidate to plant my heart inside.

After all, I am a great lover of powerful classical music.

And I was an expert conductor in my previous life – and now I can continue my great legacy of the arts in music and symphonies.

I will always have what I always wanted: a large audience to conduct my powerful symphonies to.

Also, the appearance of this middle-aged conductor who became the great heart transplant recipient of mine, is strong-featured, heavy-set and physically built like a bull as I, Domenico Armando was in his prime.

You see, my son, I married your mother five years ago in Italy.

She played the piano in the private band I conducted to all over the world.

That is how we met.

And you know, we both loved each other greatly.

And even though you and your sister Maria are not of my natural offspring, I always considered the two of you as my children and I treated you accordingly.

I gave you both everything your two hearts' desired.

I treated you both as if you were truly my flesh and blood, as Domenico Armando treated his many children in his past life.

Now unfortunately, such beautiful children of mine are all dead as your precious sister Maria is.

But let me assure you Marcus: vengeance against her dozens of killers has been forthcoming.

I executed a very beautiful poetic justice, a true justice against those filthy scums who were responsible for putting her in the grave.

I will also exact justice the same way against all the rest of my enemies throughout New York City, then the entire United States - and finally, across all four corners of this godforsaken world we live in.

My vengeance will be forever unequalled in ruthless brutality and unrelenting evil against all those I consider responsible for all lining up together, to try and bring me to my knees, not only in my former life, but the bastards of this world are still attempting to uncover my true identity - and do away with me now as they had The Great Domenico Armando previously!

But you see my son, I confide to you in things that I could not your precious sister or your beautiful mother, before she passed away last year from cervical cancer.
I lost two great women in such a short space of time who meant the world to me – and now I want sweet revenge.
Despite my great fortune gained in anonymity, I feel I am still cursed with precious losses and deaths of those I love around me as I-me-Domenico Armando was in his previous life.
I am not immune unfortunately from losing those I truly care for.
But now that I have resurrected myself via this heart transplant inside this new healthy body, I feel blessed enough to roam the streets of New York City freely, after so many years of having to remain in hiding from my enemies, particularly my number one enemy, Robert Stewart.

A man who will forever pay for his crimes
against me.

No.

Robert Stewart is not safe at all from me, no
matter what he previously thought.
And now that I have brought back the fear of
facing death at any given moment, my revenge
against him will continue on its proper course,
until his defeat is forthcoming and complete.

**Right now, I have big plans against all my
enemies!
And Robert Stewart is at the top of my list!**

He is going to pay dearly for everything he did
to me, both him and his brother who beheaded
me in a time when I was, I am sad to say,
vulnerable for the first time in my life, riddled
with sickness and terminal cancer!

Robert Stewart invaded my fortress and sent
me to the ground via that revelation – and his
brother Paul took hold of a sword and cut my
head off.

Now the heart of I-me-Domenico Armando was removed from the corpse and placed inside my new body here.

The result of that heart transplant procedure was not only successful, but also remarkable. Following that heart transplant inside this new body of mine here - every bit of anger, every recollection of my enemies' doings, and every memory of my past existence, had flooded into every cell of my new brain and body.

So now, Domenico Armando lives on and on in another body that no one on the outside knows who I am-as I know who they are!

You see, no one currently knows my true identity, not even Robert Stewart – as I know everything about them and what they did.

ESPECIALLY ROBERT STEWART!

And they cannot attack what they cannot see – meaning me – as I can and will, at any given moment, destroy their fucking lives and all their properties.
I will eliminate all their friends.
I will execute their families.
I will do all this at any time of my choosing – and they will all be powerless to stop it!

Because since they do not know who I really am, they will not know where the attacks against them are coming from.
Thus, they will not be able to stop it on time!

Not only have I chosen the perfect candidate to implant my powerful dark heart inside, but I have also chosen to recently purchase this perfect mansion in Brooklyn, situated right under the noses of everyone who is out for my blood.

And the real beauty in all this is: no one will ever be able to find me – as I can roam freely the streets of this city for the first time in years, since I previously lost my freedom as Domenico Armando.

I can plot and plan and destroy my enemies' lives – and no one will know that it is I who is The Enemy, as everyone, including my number one enemy Robert Stewart, will be powerless to stop my attacks against them.

I can go and come anonymously, whilst living in a state of anonymity, and no one will know that I, the living Maestro Dante Rolando, is

really and truly their worst fucking nightmare:
Domenico Armando!

I will bring hell and strife to all my enemies'
lives.
I will destroy their homes.
I will blow up their cars.
I will kill and destroy their friends.
I will eliminate their families.
Then I will terminate all those loathsome
people of my past with great accuracy and
daring precision.
And the world will be dumbstruck, not
knowing where all those attacks against them
are coming from.

You see, I have given Robert Stewart all the
necessary clues to know that I am back from
the dead.

**And the fear of the unknown-the fear of
uncertainty, where his life is hanging in the
balance.
The fear of facing death at any given
moment he is currently experiencing is
satisfying my soul.**

**He truly knows his life is hanging in the
balance!**

His life is surely hanging by a fucking thread. And the real fear I have caused him, is the fear of the unknown.

He knows every bit of horror and terror to be inflicted upon him shortly, will be brought on by his worst enemy: Domenico Armando.

But at the same time, I have made sure that I have left no clues behind, for him to trace me and my identity as the true culprit, he is currently rummaging through every street of this city, with his army of police friends, trying to locate and neutralise, as he had always orchestrated before, where the great mighty giant Domenico Armando is concerned.

But he will be powerless this time to not only stop me and my plans, but he also will never be able to find me.

So – first things first: My plans of destruction against Robert Stewart.
I will destroy his property.
I will destroy his family.
I will destroy his state of mind!

I will declare a war of nerves against him.

Then - I will declare the next world war against him and the police who had declared war against me and my kingdom years ago.

New York City will never be the same again!
It will soon be struck with a hell of a lot of fatalities.
A great many people are going to die, beginning in New York City and spreading throughout the whole country and the world itself!

Robert Stewart is going to pay for destroying me and my empire.
The police are going to pay for declaring war against me.

And those rats, those fucking treacherous scumbag low-class cunt politicians throughout this country, are going to pay for provoking me with their evil ways, hypocrisy, divisive policies and criminal laws, which have corrupted the land – bringing evil throughout every facet of our community, such as the book publishing industry, which resulted in the homicidal murder of my beloved daughter Maria.

You see, those fucking scumbag cunt politicians all across this country, were responsible for spreading corruption, mayhem and evil everywhere.
And they surely did not safeguard the interests of the public, such as my daughter Maria.

They never protected her from the fucking scumbags out there in this godforsaken world, who invaded her business, stealing all her royalties, leaving her deceptive untruthful bad reviews of her work, and destroyed her due to reasons of jealousy and obsession.

So, the world that is filled with such spastic and retarded fucking scumbags like this, all those bastards and bitches out there, who are everywhere – **are going to pay the severe penalty of death!**

Those fucking politicians.
Every governor and that dirty president of this nation who are all corrupt, only serving themselves, whilst damning and destroying the public and the community and their businesses – as they had my daughter Maria – are all going to pay!

Those fucking politicians, especially the governors in every state of this country and the president of this nation, are going to be targeted by my wrath!

I am going to make them all fall – and they will fall in front of everyone publicly for what they did to me and my daughter Maria!
They are all as good as dead men!

They are going to pay for all their hypocrisy and evil infractions directed towards good innocent people such as my now dead daughter Maria.

Because of her death, I am going to declare World War fucking 3.

No one of them protected her – no one saved her from those fucking cunts who wanted to sabotage her, by stealing her work.
Wanting to steal her brilliant ideas, whilst at the same time, they played games with her, terrible mind games, scarring her fragile emotions to committing suicide, as they said she was no good at her craft of writing books - and they stole all her money, millions of dollars.

These sorts of scum in this world are going to die gruesomely.

I am going to spill their blood from all parts of their bodies!

I am going to cut them all in pieces.
I will kill them.
I will kill their friends.
I will kill their husbands.
I will kill their wives.
Their pets will disappear.
I will eliminate and destroy their children – so their miserable corrupt genes will not live on and continue further corrupting generations thereafter!
I will kill their parents and I will kill their parents' parents for the sins of their ancestors!
I will terminate their co-conspirator associates in their crimes against the innocent, such as my dead daughter Maria.

The hideous politicians responsible for corrupting the land and protecting the guilty and the wicked, such as all the governors and the president of this country, are all going to die!

And then I will message Robert Stewart and I will tell him: You see all the criminals I have killed for you, Robert Stewart!

I will force you to realise that I am not the evil
demon you think I am.
But instead, I am truly an avenging angel doing
your work alongside you.

What do you think of that, Commander?
I will wipe out everyone who deserves to be
wiped out.
And all those around them are going to have
their blood spilled.
They are going to suffer.
They are going to beg me for a mercy I shall
never, never, ever grant them.
They will all die like dogs in the street!
You still want to stop me?
You still want to get me for killing scumbags,
huh Robert Stewart???

****

Within forty-eight hours later, many dead bodies began piling up in New York City. The police declared the killing spree a mass murder.

Death, doom and destruction loomed across the entire perimeters of New York State.

The Governor of the State and the deputy governor.
The vice governor.
The second-in-command.
The Lieutenant Governor.
Were both gunned down outside City Hall, during a public press conference together in the morning at 10:00 a.m.
Then the rifle gunman disappeared in the crowd, seemingly behind shadows without a trace.
He wore a large hat and sunglasses, gloves and a navy-blue jacket.
His face was concealed and hidden beneath the large hat and dark sunglasses.
So, no positive identification could be made of his identity by local witnesses to the police, who questioned them all rather quickly, as the local authorities were immediately called at the scene.

What was even worse than the public assassinations of both the Governor and the Lieutenant Governor, was that Robert Stewart had been investigating the two of those politicians for the past six weeks for corruption, right alongside the warden of one of the largest maximum-security prisons in the state, housing convicted Mob Boss, Aldo Anselmo, now for six months.

Robert Stewart had kept close tabs on Aldo Anselmo (he had arrested over six months before) – and Robert also kept close tabs on his yet active Mob clan.

He had the remainder of the Anselmo family clan on the outside under police surveillance, which included bugs, hidden cameras and phone wiretapping, in order to record their secret incriminating conversations, to nail them also, as he had their boss – and to make them share the same incarcerated fate as their murderous padrone Aldo Anselmo behind bars.

In addition to this ongoing Mob investigation, Robert Stewart also had Aldo Anselmo's prison phone calls monitored and his mail scanned – and all those inmates he was close to (used as go-between intermediaries), as well as their outside visitors Aldo Anselmo used to give and receive outside messages to and from his outside people, were all under discreet police surveillance.

In a short space of time, Robert uncovered damning evidence against the New York City Governor and his partner in crime, the Lieutenant Governor's involvement with the Mob Crime Family, the Anselmos.
And the prison warden's dirty hands were also exposed as accepting bribes from the Anselmo family.

From audio bugging and visual camera surveillance and phone wiretapping, Robert got the goods on the Governor and the Lieutenant Governor's political corruption activities and their extremely treacherous dealings in murderous criminality.

The overwhelming evidence he obtained against the Governor and the Lieutenant Governor was more than enough to not only have them impeached from office, but to have them both prosecuted in a court of law following indictments for such charges as accepting bribes, conspiracy and treason, facing prison.

Robert Stewart obtained corroborated evidence of their local and offshore secret front-controlled-and-owned bank accounts, the Anselmo family couriers deposited large six figure sums of monies inside, to assist and help convicted Mob Boss Aldo Anselmo relinquish his life sentence and return a freeman from prison.

Aldo Anselmo bribed the Governor and the Lieutenant Governor for a full pardon, based on a concocted fabricated story of phoney heroism on Aldo Anselmo's part, on behalf of the soul citizens of New York City.

Robert Stewart obtained evidence of the scam Crime Boss Aldo Anselmo finagled, to make it look as though he would forward information to the proper authorities against international terrorist threats, who planned to shell and bomb the entire city and state of New York to pieces, killing everyone who resided inside its entirety, including the police – which would secure Aldo Anselmo's pardon.

The entire story was proven a foolish scam. And the terrorists' names he would use were all a bogus sham.

There were two dying Italian hitmen in Italy, old compatriots of the Anselmo family clan.

The Anselmo family (orders of its Patriarch Aldo), also bribed the two dying Italian hitmen, to confess to a lie that they were International Terrorists, planning to bomb and machine gun all of New York City and destroy everyone in the state.

The sinister plan was for them (the two Italian hitmen) to enter New York and be found with weapons of mass destruction in their possession inside backpacks and rental flats – that would give credence and believability to their fiendish story as terrorists.

Aldo Anselmo promised to take care of their families upon their incarcerations, by providing monetary security for the rest of their lives, in exchange for the phoney story given by the two dying Italian hitmen.

One was dying from lung cancer and the other was terminal with pancreatic cancer.

In crux, Aldo Anselmo explained to his people that the hitmen were dying anyway.

So, they may as well confess and die in prison, in exchange for their families' monetary security, given to them for the rest of their lives.

Of course, Robert Stewart and his police comrades had all of the conspiracy on tape implicating Aldo Anselmo, the Governor, the Lieutenant Governor, the two dying Italian hitmen, which also incriminated over a dozen other Anselmo family mobsters – and most notably, the 'Warden's' conspired involvement in Aldo Anselmo's departure from prison, which was a backup plan in case the crime boss's initial scheme of bribing the Governor and Lieutenant Governor for a full pardon fell through.

Aldo Anselmo was also implicated in bribing the prison warden to help his people smuggle deadly explosives inside the penitentiary – and have them enter his lock up prison cell.
To have explosives planted inside his prison quarters for the sole purpose of detonation.

The warden accepted the bribes to help explode Aldo Anselmo's holding cell, making the world think that Aldo Anselmo was killed in that bomb blast inside his prison confinement at nighttime, when he was asleep.
And also, to plant phoney human remains inside the cell, prior the explosion;
Bribing certain corrupt forensic officers (mostly scientists and sworn police members), that the

blown up remains they investigated and uncovered, including bone and dental records, matched Aldo Anselmo's.

Therefore, in crux, the warden was in cahoots with the plan to plant the bomb inside the prison cell in question and have it blown to pieces.
The prison warden accepted the bribe to sneak the explosive bomb or bombs inside the prison facility.
He also equally agreed to sneak out of prison the incarcerated Mob Boss Aldo Anselmo inside the trunk of his car - and drive the convicted crime chief outside to safety at the end of his shift.
That was the backup plan.

Robert Stewart also obtained enough evidence to arrest the prison warden and two sworn police member forensic officers for charges relating to accepting bribes, their participation in mob crimes and conspiracy.

Robert also arranged to have Aldo Anselmo transferred to a more secure prison facility in the State, where he would be forced either to complete 23-hour lockdown a day and/or intense supervision.

Closer monitoring.
This time he would be allowed no visitors and contact with any of the inmates.

'But' before Aldo Anselmo's official transfer papers were finalised, and prior the ink on the numerous arrest warrants, concerning the other implicated parties involved with the Anselmo Mob had officially dried, which included separate arrest warrants with the New York City Governor and Lieutenant Governor's names written on them, the Governor and the Lieutenant Governor of the State were both assassinated outside City Hall by an unidentified assailant.
The hatchet man conveniently disappeared following plugging the two politicians with two bullets apiece in the head.

ALSO – (in case it was not an original idea or original plan or concept) - perhaps playing copycat to the idea of planting prison explosives inside the crime chief's cell, the yet invisible, unidentified, behind-the-scenes mastermind culprit **'behind'** the Governor and Lieutenant Governor's double assassinations, then 'seemingly?' borrowed the idea of smuggling and planting explosives **'for real'** (in secret), not only inside Aldo Anselmo's prison

cell, but also having a second bomb surreptitiously planted inside the warden's office.
The deadly explosives timed to detonate at the same time.
Which resulted in the deaths of both Aldo Anselmo and the prison warden.

Only the two incriminated corrupt forensic officers lived long enough for Robert Stewart to execute the official arrest orders against them.

(The two terminal hitmen in Italy were both reported dead by the Italian authorities, working in cooperation with the United States police, concerning Mob crimes affecting both their countries combined.)

The two hitmen were murdered separately inside their homes in gruesome fashion.
One had the roof of his house suddenly collapse on top of his head, crushing him to death.
The second found himself attacked by an invasion of deadly Inland Taipan snakes planted inside his house.

The snakes' venoms were extremely powerful and toxic.

The hatchet man target to the snake attacks and snake bites died a brutal death inside his small Naples flat.
The snake bites and hence poisons invading the hatchet man's central nervous system, produced convulsions and complete paralysis within only a few minutes.
Once the venoms took complete control of his body in its final stages, the dying hitman succumbed to complete respiratory paralysis and kidney failure, resulting in his death.

All in all, these series of deaths resulted in the Anselmo Mob being put out of commission and freeing New York City of major political corruption, which threatened to ruin the city, tearing it apart to pieces – and destroy all the soul citizens who resided within its perimeter walls.

In all this, Robert Stewart had a bigger problem to deal with.
He was now in a relentless crusade to hunt down the mastermind behind the murders of the two exposed corrupt chief executive of the

State and his deputy: The murdered Governor and assassinated Lieutenant Governor.
In addition to these deaths, Robert Stewart was on a wild crusade to fervently pursue and effectively locate the whereabouts of the same mastermind, also behind all the Anselmo family connected murders, which included the two eliminated Italian hatchet men, the New York prison warden and the Anselmo family chieftain.

In his heart and inside his gut, Robert Stewart only feared to consider the diabolical culprit behind the sudden mass murdering killing spree.

Robert Stewart knew this killing spree was only the beginning!

Robert Stewart also suspected the master criminal behind it all.
His old enemy, Domenico Armando.
And in order to take over and consolidate his mob power in the city, the notorious villain eliminated all his rivals, including the people those rivals had tie-ins with - such as the Governor of the State, the Lieutenant Governor and the corrupt warden and so on and so forth!

It was Domenico Armando behind it.
He was behind every bit of it.
Everything!
Now a new man: with a new identity.

Robert knew prior the old dead Domenico
Armando becoming a corpse, he previously
ordered his corrupt black heart to be implanted
inside another subject upon the end of his life.
It was for the sole purpose to live out his evil
plans and vendettas forever!
And having his heart transplanted into another
human body, was all it would take to return the
old Domenico Armando to the world!

Domenico was evil incarnate.
Every organ inside his body was tainted black.
Dark as his black soul.
So, putting his heart or any of his evil organs
inside another body, was enough for the cells of
that organ, to transmit that dark corrupt evil
into every other cell of the new head and body
it was then exposed to.
And as simple as clicking one's fingers, the
diabolical evil genius ways, evil memories and
evil persona of Domenico Armando would
continue to radiate inside another body.

That heart transplant recipient would instantly become possessed by Domenico Armando's organ donation – and he would automatically become an exact duplicate of Domenico himself!

Robert, in himself, had to uncover the identity of that heart transplant recipient and very soon, or else more deaths would ensue, and all hell would break loose.

That would surely result in tearing, smashing and destroying the entire city and state of New York.

Which would also result in innocent civilians (following his further ordered mass slaughterhouse killings) next time, being caught in the crossfire of Domenico Armando's mass murdering inflicted lunacy!

****

Robert Stewart at present in the month of December in the year 1997, had been investigating all heart transplant recipients and heart transplant surgeries, which took place in the state of New York at around the time of Domenico's death all those years ago, on the 23rd of March 1991.

But what made it close to impossible to trace the correct heart transplant recipient of Domenico's heart, was that the surgery was not performed officially inside any legitimate hospital by any recognised legitimate practising doctor.

Whereby in ordinary circumstances, records of heart transplants were logged and documented in patient histories properly.

And such medical records in local doctor offices and public or private hospital institutions, could be also legally checked by police.

No.

Domenico Armando's heart donation operation into some unidentified transplant recipient was all performed out of sight, under the radar.

All under the table.

No records found anywhere through legitimate means.

In crux, Domenico Armando was a very wealthy man, with extensive hidden funds all over the world.
He also had an unlimited supply of international connections.
That meant – secret underground hospital facilities, with mob doctors, who all practised unofficially, off the scope - and without maintaining official record-keeping medical documents for anyone, especially those of the police variety, to track!

So, Robert was going to have to be a bit more resourceful in his search for clues to the identity of his diabolical master enemy, the dark villainous magician Domenico Armando was always known to be.

Robert Stewart suspected Domenico Armando was situated in the city of New York hiding somewhere, concealed safely in his new identity, whoever that was.
And wherever that person was residing allegedly within the city limits.

Robert Stewart was one law-enforcement official who thought outside the box.

He would not allow the police rule book to dictate his actions, unlike what he was taught at the police academy.
But he would broaden his scope and improvise whenever necessary in order to solve a difficult case such as this one.

In a nutshell, Robert had to orchestrate certain cross-reference checks matching the MO of the mass murderer they (the police), were fervently hunting at present - (meaning Domenico Armando in disguise).

Domenico Armando was a homicidal lunatic. He was a monstrous and barbaric mass murderer.

That was the clue!
That was the MO!

Robert thought to himself: we just had a string of mass disappearances only recently!

This string of disappearances happened at the same time.
All of them were orchestrated across many sections of the country, not just New York alone.

These '97' people were all filed nationally inside the police 'Missing Persons List'.

But were they just missing?
Or were they kidnapped and summoned all together, murdered and then forced to disappear?

What was the connection?
What was the pattern which leads to a single solid clue behind the disappearances of all those people, which occurred at approximately the same time across over two dozen different states throughout the country?

Robert Stewart was situated inside his Brooklyn-based 25th division precinct station house office, investigating solid leads on his police computer.
The one common denominator of all these missing (suspected murdered) men and women, was that they were all either brick-and-mortar bookstore operators and proprietors, or its employees.
And that number included a book printing proprietor with managers and employees, but the printing aspect was NOT situated across many different states throughout the country (unlike the bookstore operatives).

Only one printing facility of personnel was targeted: just a single New York City business.

Ok.
That was the common denominator.
But why? – Robert thought out loud to himself.
Why have they disappeared or why were they murdered at the same time?
They have all been taken out, removed from circulation without a trace.
Again - why?
What was the motive for this suspected mass murder?
We can skip opportunity for now.
Domenico, as sick and resourceful as he is, has an unlimited amount of manpower and resources and ample opportunity to kill someone – and many people – if he wants to.
Right now, the most important piece of the puzzle to solve this case is: **'motive!'**
What was the motive for the suspected mass murder of all these bookstore and book printing operators and workers?
This is certainly a coincidental mass disappearance.
Or intentional kidnapping and mass murder.

This is certainly the MO of a tyrant behind this.

Someone with a lot of money and power who can organise such attacks at the same time all across different states of the country.

This is certainly the MO of only one man who comes to mind, as capable of such an organised mass attack, in over two dozen states in this country at the same time, next to Adolf Hitler. And that man is: Domenico Armando!

But why?
Why would he kill those people?
What have they done to him?
How did they provoke this mass attack against them?

Domenico was a maniac for sure, but he was not someone who would kill a large number of people indiscriminately, for no valid reason in his mind.
He would not attack masses of people like this, unless he had a very good reason.

I have to keep digging for answers.
If I can find out the motive for these mass disappearances-suspected mass murders, then I will be very close to uncovering the identity of our man here.

I will know once and for all who this enemy is.
Come on.
Think, Robert!
Keep searching for clues.
Keep digging for answers on your police computer.
What is the link between all these suspected deaths and Domenico Armando?

Already I have established the MO.
It is a mass disappearance.
Suspected mass murder.
This is Domenico's style.
It is definitely his trademark!
And the opportunity for all these crimes needs no further explanation where Domenico is concerned.
He always has ample opportunity to kill whoever he chooses to kill.
But there has to be a reason.
That's the true motive.
What the hell is the reason?

I have to keep searching for answers.
I have to keep digging for clues.
I have to find the answers to these important questions, or else Domenico's killing sprees will no doubt target a great many civilians caught in the crossfire.

Ok.

Let's investigate possible clues, leads and reasons for the true 'motive' behind all these disappearances of these subjects – and/or their murders.

Robert kept pursuing leads on his police computer, until he came across a recently reported suicide in the city, of a first-time young female book writer named Maria Romeo.
Robert investigated her history on the police database computer records.
Her natural father Mario Romeo was Italian, born in Rome before migrating to the United States at the age of thirty.
He was a car mechanic and an alcoholic, who died ten years ago from alcohol poisoning at the age of fifty-two.
Maria's mother Vanessa Romeo also died last year from cervical cancer.
But before she died, she was a professional piano player for many years.
She remarried five years ago to a man named, Dante Rolando.
He was also a famous conductor.
Perhaps that was how his wife met him, as she played the piano.

Ok.

So, what would be the likely connection?
Think, Robert, think!

We have dozens of suspected dead bookstore owners and employees across the nation and one suspected dead New York-based book printer owner, including its workers - and not long before that, we had a book writer who lived in this city who committed suicide.
And her mother was a piano player.
But she is now dead.
And her stepfather is a famous conductor.

Robert clenched and unclenched his jaw several times, almost grinding his teeth, as he tried to put the pieces of this puzzle together.
He thought long and hard about the possibilities.

Then snap!
His mind began to work perfectly right now as always in the past, the great cop he was described by all his colleagues to be;
The great cop Robert Stewart who had naturally inspired his entire police department to be admittedly 'mighty proud to be cops!'

My God!

Sweet mother of Jesus!
Robert thought to himself in horror.
My God! – he said out loud this time.

He thought another grave thought or two
currently in terror.
Maria Romeo's stepfather was a conductor.
Domenico liked to conduct privately.
Wait a minute…!
I have to investigate further.
Is it possible that this conductor had a heart
transplant at the time of Domenico's death all
those years ago?
But something tells me, even if he did, it would
have been done surreptitiously, off the radar, all
unofficially.
And any hospital I question in this city in order
to obtain access to their medical files of
suspected heart transplant recipients, dating
back to that period, would turn out a dead-end
anyway.
My guess is, that Domenico's heart transplant
recipient would have had that operation in
secret, all unofficially, in no legitimately
registered hospital, with no legitimate registered
doctor.
Meaning – no official medical records of that
particular operation would ever be found in any
and all hospital records searched by police

citywide, even should the hospital administrators each be subpoenaed to supply all hospital records to that effect for legal perusal. Also meaning evidence to the sighting of that particular surgery.

But Robert was thorough as well as effective in his policing role.
He spent the next few days searching every private and public hospital in the city.

Unfortunately, 'no' records of a heart transplant being obtained by a conductor named Dante Rolando were ever recorded.
Which still meant, the operation could have taken place on the recipient in question, the heart transplant that was.
But as Robert suspected, it was not performed officially in any legitimate operational hospital facility.
It was all done off the books.
No records kept.

Damn it! Robert growled after his intensive city-wide hospital investigations turned out no solid leads.
I need answers and quick.
I have to find out the truth.

Regardless of any official hospital records found or not found, this conductor is the one solid piece of information – and the one solid piece of the puzzle and definite clue I have found, since Armando's corrupt doctor (whoever he is), sent me that letter, now three weeks ago.

I have to investigate this so-called conductor, Dante Rolando.
And we have to be very careful and discreet about it.
There can be no leaks of this investigation, especially to the press.
No reporters must know what we are doing.
Everything must remain hush-hush!
Completely confidential!

Domenico or Dante, if they are one in the same, must not find out that we are investigating him.

As our target has remained invisible to us all this time – so too must I and the police movements against him remain imperceptible.
Our target must not be tipped off of our intention or our investigation into his private affairs, or else if he is Domenico, he will conspire to do another disappearing act on us.

And we cannot afford to lose sight of him again – or else a great many lives are going to be lost; I fear many of those could be civilian lives if we are not careful and keep a tight lid on our investigation – now against Maestro Dante Rolando!

I have a feeling this is not going to be easy. And this is going to take time for us to come up with the proper answers.

We have to investigate thoroughly the connection between the bookstore companies and book printer facility - and any possible link with Dante Rolando, and possibly his dead writer stepdaughter.

Were they in business together?

Did their business turn sour?

Our investigations into these two separate entities must include checks on bank account records.

Did Dante and these many bookstore companies and one printing company have any possible monies changing hands?

And if so, did any of these bookstore retailers and book printing facility operators steal any money from Maria, perhaps her books sales, royalties, compensations and revenues?

Was that the reason for their disappearances and possible mass murders at the hands of

Domenico Armando-suspected-Dante Rolando?

Immediate police investigations will be conducted, beginning with checking all bank records of Dante Rolando and these missing bookstore and book printing operatives' personal and business bank accounts, to determine any possible monetary transaction tie-ins between the three of them. And to determine if any money was stolen, which would most certainly pinpoint a true motive behind their suspected mass killings!

Regardless, we need to get our man: Domenico Armando!

But in order to do that, an official thorough police investigation is now warranted against Dante Rolando.

And if he is **'The Enemy'** - once I get my hands on him, I am going to make him pay for all his past mass murders - and all those killing sprees in the not-so-distant future he plans to commit, once Domenico Armando becomes my prisoner again!

****

As part of his full-scale police investigation currently underway, Commander Robert Stewart immediately ordered his policemen the following commands inside his station house precinct: We have a very dangerous homicidal maniac roaming around the city, a mass murderer!

You know our target!

I want every police officer in this city to be extra careful!

And don't let anyone exit this city until you thoroughly check that person out.

Especially if that person happens to be Conductor Dante Rolando.

So, watch your backs and each other's - your police partners and colleagues – and everyone else's you come into contact with.

Now, let me say this for the record: our target's name is, Dante Rolando.

Right now, he is our number one suspect in the Armando case.

And I repeat: no one leaves this city without our permission!

Meaning: Dante Rolando.

So, get a move on!

I want tight lips on all our movements, especially from the press.
No leaks to any newspaper people!
And no reporters are allowed to lurk anywhere inside here within the walls of this station house!
If they are spotted, and they don't leave when asked, then arrest them!

I want this entire city and all its exits sealed off!
The waterfront and harbour areas, the bus depots, the train stations and commercial and private air terminals – I want them all watched extra carefully.
I want roadblocks set up, covering all entrances and exits in and out of this city – major and otherwise.
Meaning - all major roads and highways through to every backstreet and alleyway – everything covered!

No one sneaks out of New York without us knowing about it!
I want this entire city locked up tight!!!

We have established reasonable suspicion against Dante Rolando, we suspect matches the profile and MO of our target!

And I want immediate full-scale surveillance planted on Maestro Dante Rolando.
I want to know for sure if he is 'The Enemy' we are looking for.
I want to know if he is Domenico Armando. And if he is, I want him off the streets!

In the meantime, until we verify the truth of our target's identity, that Conductor, Dante Rolando, is not permitted to leave our sight for even one second!

So, for now: we watch and we wait!

And if our enemy wants a war, then a war is exactly what we are going to give him!

PART THREE

The New York City Police Department had declared war against all the major criminals throughout the entire State.

And Police Commander Robert Stewart was leading his extensive police troops into the battlefield, against all its menacing enemy targeted threats.

The great problem the police faced at present, was that their main targets comprised of extremely despicable men who in fact wore important titles within the inner circles of society.

They were dishonourable and disreputable men who each carried honourable and reputable titles.

Their three main targets were: Conductor Dante Rolando, The Archbishop of New York City and the President of the United States.

Firstly: Conductor Dante Rolando:

He was suspected mass murderer Domenico Armando.

What progress had the police made against him concerning their investigation so far?

Robert Stewart uncovered solid evidence of the Dante Rolando's bank records. Both personal and business.

Robert uncovered monetary transactions between Dante and the suspected dead 97 national bookstore owners and/or its employees, and one New York City book printing company proprietor and staff members.

Dante Rolando had purchased over a million copies of his dead stepdaughter Maria's book from the book printing company in New York - and distributed those books to the mentioned missing nationwide (suspected dead) bookstore retailers. The personnel.

The police investigation into this trio (of Dante Rolando, the bookstores and the New York City printer), uncovered evidence that the New York City printing company and consecutive nation-wide bookstore retailers, had ripped off Dante and his stepdaughter Maria. And thus, not only had the suspected culprits vanished from circulation, but also bank records indicated that their monies both earned and stolen, were also robbed from them via fronts (suspected controlled by Dante), but unfortunately so far, not traced to him.

Robert was thoroughly investigating those fronts in order to connect them to Dante Rolando.

Nonetheless, the police were able to pinpoint the direct link and solid connection between their number one suspect Dante, and the missing monetary fortunes of all the presumed dead bookstore outlets and the one book printing company's specific targeted workers. Also, the police tied Dante to their prior disappearances and suspected mass murders. It was a real solid tie-in of the trio.

With the main exception being an act of malice (and sometimes quite often, the desire of **'malice'** and a state of maliciousness, being the additional inclusive driving force behind acts of premediated and random acts of murder) – but that aside, in many instances, in order to solve a criminal case, the police required **motive and opportunity.** In the case of Dante and his stepdaughter's rip-off and Maria's consecutive suicide, Dante Rolando satisfied the curiosity of the police on those main fronts. Even the instance of **malice** was suspected by their targeted man, in the carrying out of his acts of brutal torture and cold-and-calculated mass slaughter of all the mentioned victims. It was strongly believed that if Dante Rolando was truly behind their deaths, such mass killings would have been orchestrated in an exceptionally brutal and sadistic fashion, given the nature of the unconscionable crimes they committed against his stepdaughter Maria – and her subsequent suicide as a result of those crimes committed against her.

And if Dante was in fact Domenico, the MO (modus operandi) of all such suspected deaths, was surely established on that front as well; such a mass murderer being capable of committing such barbaric acts on such a grand scale.

Also, Robert Stewart uncovered solid evidence as he investigated necessary medical records, that Dante Rolando, who was alleged to be Domenico Armando, never had heart problems. And that answered a very curious question to Robert. Was the heart transplant surgery consented or was it forced? If Dante was in fact their true enemy Domenico, then the heart transplant surgery was surely forced.

At the time when Domenico Armando was still alive, Dante Rolando in fact was married to an Italian wife and they had one son together whom, if lived, would have been twenty years old today.

But over six years ago (at the time of Domenico's death), both Dante's wife and son were reported killed in a private plane crash. It was reported to be an accident. But the sheer coincidence of their deaths and Domenico's death occurring at approximately the same time, allowing for the road to remain clear for Domenico's forced heart transplant procedure into Dante's chest, without his family's interference, proved greatly suspicious to Robert as well as coincidental.

In addition to these matters, Robert constantly checked his home and vehicle for possible surveillance devices planted by the enemy. So far, his privacy was not being invaded, nor his movements being monitored by the enemy. But that did not mean the enemy may not attempt future surveillance on him. Regardless, Robert would constantly safeguard against any and all possible eavesdropping and hidden camera devices being planted inside and around his domain and territory by his target man, by regularly conducting a sweep of his properties. And meanwhile taking extra precautions to ensure that his movements and investigation against his target remained top secret!

Robert Stewart had big plans for Dante Rolando in order to obtain all the information he needed against him. And if Dante Rolando was his true enemy Domenico Armando, Robert would establish all the evidence he needed through infiltrating his enemy's fortress. He was going to infiltrate his enemy's camp by initiating an elaborate undercover operation inside his home to not only get close to Dante, but to also use his entrance inside his home to snoop around and see for himself what deep dark secrets Rolando was hiding, in order to expose them. And if Dante was his man, Robert planned to not only expose that information, all the incriminating information against him, but to hang him with that evidence!

As the police were patrolling the city streets in search for clues against their target named Dante Rolando, one team of plainclothes surveillance officers led by Robert Stewart, uncovered an arms dealer accepting an initial down payment from a customer, for an illegal order of arms verbally discussed between them down at the docks – and the arms dealer (unaware of the inconspicuous danger around him), unsuspectingly led the police to an industrial unit. It was a gun factory in Brooklyn.

Just before the police entered, they heard gunshots inside of manufactured guns being tested. Within 30 seconds of the test firing, the police stormed the entire building on grounds of reasonable suspicion. That police interception led to the arrests of eighteen men and six women working inside the illegal gun manufacturing complex, in the borough of Brooklyn.

A handful of the apprehended illegal arms manufacturers chose to run instead of being arrested. Some of them carelessly opened fire on the police who were instantly cut down by armed officers - and those criminals who ran found themselves cut-off rather quickly by extensive police troops who surrounded the entire vicinity of the area. It was either drop their weapons and surrender or be shot.

Most surrendered without any fuss. Some chose the idiotic action of fighting the police. And those illegal arms workers became sorry individuals who resulted in being shot dead, in what was extremely swift police action against them, resulting in the villains' sudden fatalities via self-defence.

What police uncovered inside this industrial unit was that it was an illicit factory for both hand and machine guns.

It was the largest, most unprecedented manufacturer of illegal weapons discovered throughout the entire country.

The gun factory was occupied by equipment and people for the sole purpose of manufactory illegal deadly weapons for sale and distribution illegally, to vast legions of criminals so they could be used to kill people.

The manager of the place was called Mr. Pusher. He was a large, fat, middle-aged, odd-looking man, wearing a large navy-blue suit and red tie. He wore a large dark blue hat matching the colour of his suit and he had shoulder-length red, mixed with salt-and-pepper colour hair - and a lengthy salt-and-pepper mixed with red-coloured moustache and beard. He was also arrested. And the police frisked him and found in his personal possession, two illegal handguns stuffed inside his blazer pocket.

Regardless, the much taken-by-surprise Mr. Pusher was just a front man for someone much bigger controlling the illegal arms trade in the city. Robert immediately suspected Dante Rolando behind this operation.

This factory was new in town. So was Dante.

The police spent many days thoroughly searching the very large gun factory and confiscated all the equipment, gun component parts and the hundreds of finished product illegal weapons manufactured inside the extensive complex.

The handguns and machine guns confiscated were of high calibre; easily capable of killing a group of people on both small and large scales.

The weapons were handmade from bits of metal, but they were very lethal barrel weapons, just as deadly and dangerous as any other arms manufacturing industry across the globe.

The guns confiscated inside the Brooklyn complex were guns which were prohibited; very powerful lethal firearms, including machine guns and submachine guns. These weapons were certainly prohibited to be owned by any civilian across the state. And the criminals operating inside this complex were not only manufacturing the weapons, but also making them available to be purchased by any interested person or persons for the sole purpose of killing individuals - or many groups of people either at random or a premeditated fashion.

The guns confiscated were not only lethal, but they were untraceable. They contained no serial numbers.

Upon the arrests of all the criminals operating inside the complex, the illegal arms factory was immediately closed down after being raided by the police!

The police and district attorney built a very strong case for the prosecution of all those involved with the illegal weapons factory industry.

The hefty sentences received by the culprits matched the gravity of their crimes in producing illegal and prohibited deadly weapons, with intent to sell them to the general public for the purposes of murder and mass murder! To kill people on both small and large scales!

Robert Stewart suspected the culprit behind this very large national and international illegal arms ring was none other than Dante Rolando. And the arrested so-called owner and manager of the illegal weapons factory, Mr. Pusher, was just a front man. Robert's hunch was that even this front man would rather die in prison than rat on his boss.

Robert now had possession of all the illegal arms factory's secret inventory, including its customers globally who ordered illegal deadly weapons from the Brooklyn complex. Robert instantly planned to hunt them down. His main targets were certain Italian underworld crime family chieftains, who were direct international associates and business partners with those United States syndicate leaders, in the international illegal drugs and arms import-export business!

The Italian crime families in question whom the currently incarcerated Mr. Pusher had supplied his deadly arms to, were some of the worst armies of killers across the entire globe. The syndicate families were extremely deadly mass murders of innocent civilians, even the Italian police who were investigating them. They were very deadly, very dangerous menacing terrorists, who threatened both Italian and American lives just by their existences.

Robert Stewart and his extremely powerful international crime-fighting unit he was affiliated with, known as the SIA, were in one mind concerning those international mass murdering terrorists: they had to be stopped in whatever forceful means necessary.

And that meant: going to war. Waging war against those who threatened their lives. It would be a war of blood and guts.

In order to win a war against brutal killers - one had to exact the principle of: **TOTAL ANNIHILATION!**
The only way to defeat an enemy of deadly proportions was to destroy that foe. To annihilate all of them! To kill everyone from the head to the foot. That meant killing the boss right to the lowest-ranked soldier. Waging war against underworld terrorists was a battle of annihilation. There was no other way! The strategy was simple. To engage in a powerful air attack and drop hundreds and thousands of bombs over all of them from warplanes - and/or advancing one's armies towards them on foot - and fire your more superior weapons and deadly artillery causing direct havoc. You amass your best-trained armies and ensure your side had the most men (or availability of masses of standby manpower at your disposal) - and most powerful arms - and you strike first whilst outgunning and/or outnumbering the opposing force. It would need to be a crippling blow! To become a war of shoot to kill. **The goal was simple: total destruction of the evil opponent! To engage the enemy force and**

destroy his morale. Going toe-to-toe in what would be: a battle of annihilation! That was the one strategic feat of military brilliance required! To successfully lay siege against the adversary. To 'outnumber and outgun' the enemy in direct military action! And keep harassing the targets by bombarding the enemy units with deadly arsenal, in a war of attrition, without allowing the enemy and enemies a chance to rest and recoup! It was the only way to crush him! To crush them all on the battlefield! To kill them all first as efficiently, accurately, aggressively as possible - so you could minimise and preserve casualties of the Allies!

Robert became a master strategist who planned to destroy the enemy targets by constantly attacking them successfully. By kicking their arses one by one and altogether, so they had no time to retaliate, to rest - even to replenish their energy reserves by eating or drinking. To lead the task force into the successful war and keep constant pressure on the enemy opponents, so they had no chance to do anything about it. So, the opposing force could not surround them or outnumber them or outgun them. To keep the pressure on the targets' day and night, until they were all destroyed. At the end of the day, either the enemies all die with its cohorts in the quickest period of time possible - or the enemies kill them-the good guys! There was no choice. To minimise casualties and save innocent lives, then the enemy and its army or armies of men had to be stopped cold through **'total annihilation!'**

Robert Stewart understood the real cold heart truth of the matter perfectly. He suspected Dante Rolando as the mastermind behind all the crimes of the two worlds. Meaning: the Italian-American alliance. So, to destroy his power economically, the proper authorities not only had to crackdown on the Mafioso's power domestically throughout the United States regions, such as the raid on his illegal weapons manufacturing industry – but, at the same time, to destroy his criminal international ties he was in business with; who were feeding his coffers through their illegal and dangerous import-export trades together.

Robert and his SIA International Crime-Fighting Unit, sent its Allied forces into Sicily, targeting the menacing mob families on that island, who were currently at war with the police for total control of that region.

Robert and his armed SIA comrades outlined their plans whilst holding maps of the entire Sicilian targeted areas, to launch a successful attack against the crime bosses and its thousands of soldiers, who were situated on several various large acreages of lands they occupied in the area.

This was the moment the SIA had been waiting for. To eliminate international criminals who threatened not only their Italian police allies in Italy, but also threatened the lives of those law-enforcement officials on American soil.

The SIA sent over a thousand-armed agents to storm Sicily's criminal empires. Leading the charge for the powerful crime-fighting unit was their top agent, Robert Stewart.

He was a man who had one main goal in mind at present: to destroy the return of the evil Domenico Armando by destroying all his international ties who contributed to his evil power, influence and monetary riches.

Domenico Armando was a powerful man. But Robert Stewart was also a powerful man with an extraordinary aura who had the genius skills of not only policing great wins for his fellow local police department, but he was also considered the top agent in his international crime-fighting unit, the SIA.

And Robert Stewart's extraordinary power was derived by his natural ability to inspire his own men to be completely loyal to the objective of neutralising the opposition.

The local New York City Police Department and the SIA knew Robert's record as law-enforcement cop and secret agent. They knew that by following his lead, results would happen faster and better – and most importantly: - **they were going to win!!! And they were going to win because they were working with a winner!!!**

Robert Stewart arrived in Sicily with over a thousand SIA armed soldiers ready to demolish the enemies.

He was going to seize the Sicilian Capital Palermo by sheer force of will. Robert studied the map of the entire areas where the underworld targets and its masses of soldiers occupied, threatening all of Italy and responsible for the murder of thousands of civilians and masses of law-enforcement personnel.

In the eyes of the SIA, they had to be stopped by whatever means necessary.

114

Robert Stewart and the SIA launched a great assault against the powerful underworld terrorists occupying Palermo.

Sweeping around the targets in their army greens, armed with powerful weapons, they opened fire against the enemy in the nick of time just as they were spotted. They shot them in masses before the terrorists could strike at them first.

The proper authorities conducted their war against the enemies first on foot in order to rescue Sicily and its Capital from extremely dangerous narcissistic mass murderers, who took control of the areas, threatening to kill anyone who posed as pitfalls to their everyday conduct of business in illegal drugs, illegal arms, extortion, underaged sex slavery and killing any proper police, politician, prosecutor and judges who were seen as dangers to them.

Robert Stewart and his SIA soldiers were ready to launch a massive attack against the Italian criminal allegiance to the United States underworld forces.

The Allied armies moved in for the kill, shooting down the Palermo underworld fiends with heavy artillery, smashing them to pieces. Blowing away their heads and crushing their bodies, blasting away through their flesh with their ammunition shots fired and crushing all their bones that occupied their entire beings. From crushed skulls to crushed feet. No bone was spared and no part of their bodies was blood free.

The SIA troops were killing the underworld soldiers in fantastic fashion; very expediently.

As the SIA eliminated the underworld terrorists, Italy became free from such mob control. City by city was being freed from such dictatorial tyranny which had threatened to take over and control all its businesses, its civilians, its politicians, prosecutors, judges – even the police were being eliminated daily as part of the underworld's extensive control plans of the entire country of Italy.

Now the country and its main targeted island Sicily were being freed from this evil dark spell which consumed them for so many years. And they were being freed via this effective gunbattle initiated right away by the Allies of the Italian proper authorities against the narcissistic underworld terrorists who threatened to destroy the country-but entirely.

NOW the underworld chiefs hiding inside their villas across Sicily were forced to watch their empires crumble, just as they were forced to witness their manpower and resources put to death, as efficiently as such criminal underworld chieftains had previously ordered such murdering soldiers to in fact kill and plunge hundreds and thousands of innocent people into their graves for them.

Hence, the tables were turned. And the killers were being killed. Thus, the victims were no longer able to be threatened by them.

Once the SIA foot soldiers had cleared the area far away for cover and safety, the next phase of the plan was cast forward and shockingly unleashed immediately.

Finally, to finish off the remainder of the hidden mobsters and their bosses inside their villas across Palermo, Robert Stewart and the SIA constructed a full-blown final campaign of awe-inspiring total destruction, against every black-hearted member of the Italian criminal regimes using heavy bombers.

Squadrons of American air power fighter bomber planes were brought into the city of Palermo, combing the entire Mob-controlled and mob-dominated occupied areas, flying above the targeted lands with orders for the final attack.

This was Operation Clobber. And the word **'Clobber'** was used in its entire three favoured dictionary meanings: 'to deliver a blow to (someone or something) usually in a strong vigorous manner'. And: 'to hit someone or something hard and repeatedly'. Also: 'to defeat overwhelmingly'.

Operation Clobber became a well-constructed carpet-bombing mission by the American Allies against its Italian underworld threats.

Operation Clobber was designed to provide an opening for the SIA against the Italian underworld terrorists, thus finally eliminating the stalemate.

Operation Clobber deployed these strategic fighter bombing planes to fly into the mob-controlled areas in Sicily, known as their strike zone and strike zones - and completely destroy that mob-controlled strike zone with every bomb those fighter planes carried. The entire areas and all the buildings with all its criminal Mafioso terrorist rulers and the remainder of their hidden soldiers and evil mass murderers and spree killers, would instantly be completely obliterated and killed, once the masses of bombs released from the flying planes above had landed on top of them, ripping into their domains, erupting as shocking fireballs, killing all the horrible people in the terrible blasts.

The targets were all the tyrannical Mafia chiefs in the areas and the remainder of their mass murdering soldier people.

The ground shook violently and the land had vibrated gruesomely as the dropped bombs had landed. It was an earth-shattering firestorm for the criminal dictators and their mass murdering soldiers across the large areas of lands they occupied in the city of Palermo.

The tactics and strategy by the SIA were to completely kill and destroy the enemy threats, by dropping mass numbers of bombs over their heads, before they could kill any of them, including many more countless civilian lives across Italy.

The results were the complete obliteration of the targeted Italian Mafia crime chiefs situated across Palermo, and all their people. As the bombs struck below, the ground was shaking terribly, as the many bomb blasts exploded everywhere around the extensively large criminal-occupied land acreages, consuming everything in sight, buildings and life form.

Everything was gone. Evil empires and their wicked owners had instantly disappeared once the many bombs struck the earth around them. Their homes and empires were completely shattered and destroyed. Brick and tile were brought crumbling down to rubble. And all life forms of evil human beings were also turned to ash.

Dante Rolando was forced to watch his Italian allies being slaughtered, killed and overthrown in shame, embarrassment and disgrace. And Dante Rolando knew that Robert Stewart and his allies were coming for him next!

Secondly: The New York City Police Department Versus The Enemy Crime Family:

Two nights' later, the incarcerated Mr. Frank Pusher's twin brother Scott Pusher was busted on drug dealing and heroin drug possession charges; he was also charged with carrying an unlicenced illegal firearm and attempted murder charges of two arresting police officers on the New York City Bronx Borough Waterfront Dock 34.

Mr. Scott Pusher had resisted arrest whilst attempting to shoot two arresting police officers at the scene, who returned his action via a swift reaction of shooting him in self-defence. He died momentarily thereafter.

Robert Stewart was notified of this bust of the illegal drug dealing second brother of the Pusher clan - and congratulated the Bronx police at their swift action. It seemed as though the police were doing their job extraordinarily well. The extensive police patrols combing the streets of New York City in a bid to locate and smash the Mob's operations was working like clockwork.

The Rolando Mob Family was quickly being stripped of their power in the city, as well as their influence, as all their key people were not only being apprehended, but they were all being busted by the police patrols out on the street rather effectively!

It was now business as usual for Robert Stewart inside his local Brooklyn Police Department, 25th division precinct station house in New York.

And now with the confirmed death of the second Pusher sibling named Scott, Robert had orchestrated an elaborate plan to use that death to his advantage.

Quite rapidly, Robert informed his police patrols stationed in the Bronx, as well as the police chief commissioners in every precinct of the entire State of New York, to keep the death details of Scott Pusher a secret from the press; even his arrest that led to his death. Robert wanted to use that particular identity 'Scott Pusher' to infiltrate the Mob. To get to the higher-ups inside the organisation, until they could effectively climb the ladder of the criminal hierarchy and locate the Big Boss; Robert strongly suspected that crime chief's name to be none other than, Dante Rolando.

Robert was going to disguise himself rather cleverly as Scott Pusher and use that disguise to infiltrate the Mob.

Inside his police station office that night, Robert revealed himself to his best friend and police partner, Captain John McCallum.

John was baffled as he witnessed his police partner Robert expertly disguised by a special police make-up artist (for various disguises), who fitted him with a wig and moustache and beard, with the same unusual clothes the Pusher brothers wore. Robert also had his body bulked up with cushions and fabric to make his body look as overweight and hefty, matching Scott's obese weight in appearance.

John was almost shocked as he witnessed what appeared to be the identical twin brother of the incarcerated Frank Pusher, named Scott.

Robert hinted, "This is how we're going to get to them expediently, partner. With this disguise, I am going to walk the streets and come into contact with those Mob guys, until I get the names of all parties involved, including the man behind it all. So, we can nail every one of them!"

Robert soon after got a call at the station house. The time was a tad after midnight. It was his father Carl Stewart who reported a tragic disaster down at his fish market business on the Brooklyn waterfront, requiring the police services of his son immediately.

Robert Stewart had quickly removed his disguise and dressed himself with his plainclothes attire as he served the police as a plainclothes cop - and rapidly made his way down to his father's fish market business at the waterfront with his police partner John inside his unmarked car. And an army of uniformed police followed them inside their marked police vehicles, ready to investigate the deadly serious emergency which had befallen the Stewart family at this exact moment in time.

As soon as Robert arrived at his parents' fish market with his police partner John, he witnessed the mass murderous sight before him inside the front door of his father's small business.

Robert quickly consoled his parents who were shellshocked. His mother Julie was weeping terribly and appeared extremely shaken as his father spoke to Robert to explain what he experienced: "Your mother and I were upstairs in our room sleeping. Then your mother woke up to make us both some hot cocoa, when she witnessed this horror before us. Then I was startled by her sudden screams and that's when I ran down here and immediately called the station house to ask for your assistance!"

"You did good, Pop," Robert said serious-faced. "Don't worry. I'll take care of everything. You both will be safe now. I'll get to the bottom of this and we'll get the culprit or culprits responsible. I promise you!"

His father continued: "We didn't touch anything until you police people got here. Not to tamper with any evidence. Look at all this blood everywhere. The place looks like a bloodbath. Who would do such a thing to us? Why would they do such a thing like this. And why us?"

As Robert comforted his startled parents, his police partner John with a team of police officials began investigating the bloody mass murder which took place inside the Stewart parents' fish market business.

Initially on the surface, it would appear as though there was no forced entry, no doors broken, no windows smashed. But upon commencing their thorough police investigation, evidence found the front door locks were expertly picked and opened. The door locks seemed damaged where keys were ordinarily inserted. The killer assassins forced their way inside the building after shooting everyone in sight around them who otherwise blocked their path. The three police officers who were assigned to guard the Stewart parents were shot to death each in the chest and head outside the premises. The trail of blood on the concrete path outside had stretched onto the hardwood flooring of the fish market, where the three dead bodies were intentionally dragged inside, in order to scare the entire Stewart family, possibly to death! And amongst the three dead police corpses, was the gruesome sight of a dead orangutan lying on its back with a large butcher knife stuck into its chest. There was blood everywhere which had poured out from the major knife wound of the great ape, also found dead onto the floor of their small business.

John ordered his present police team: "I want you to do a thorough investigation here. I want you to go through this entire place inch by inch. Get the police forensics lab boys over here. And get on the phone and call some more reinforcements. I want extra 24-hour police guards placed on all members of the Stewart family. Tell the cavalry to get their tails over here on the double, pronto! And I want the personal security in this place overhauled. This must never be allowed to happen again! I want more manpower and surveillance equipment installed on all the entrances to this place, so we can monitor every threat at all hours of the day! No threat is going to be able to get anywhere near this place ever again! I want the police to investigate everything inside this building and I want the outside perimeters all checked out. And that means everywhere within a ten-mile radius all around this fish market, so we can establish clues as to who was responsible for these four killings! Question the neighbours and any potential local witnesses to see if they saw anything, even remotely suspicious lurking around the waterfront area at and around the estimated time of these murders. I want everything that can be done, done…the works. And call all the police guards assigned to the protection of the remainder of the Stewart family. Make sure they are all ok. So, get to it. And keep me posted of everything you find out!"

The officers dutifully went to work.

Robert knew who was responsible for this bloody atrocity committed inside his parents' fish market business residence. Since he found out that Domenico was back, he assigned police guards on all members of his family. Robert knew Domenico was behind the brutal murders of the three uniformed police officers and this dead great ape dragged inside the walls of the building.

Robert knew the war with his real number one enemy was not over. It never was. The war in fact was just beginning. That son of a bitch Domenico was supposed to be out of all their lives forever. He was supposed to be long gone. He was dead. He was confirmed dead years ago. But that evil genius maniacal monster deranged lunatic managed to get one over on them again by returning from the grave to begin or continue his mass murdering killing sprees left and right, scaring everyone to death - and causing chaos, mayhem and destruction in the world at large furthermore.

The bastard was supposed to be dead. One of the worst criminals the world has ever seen and faced was supposed to be in the grave out of their lives for good. But now that sick and evil maniac had returned to haunt them from even his grave. And at exactly this moment, his entire family was caught in the middle of this extremely lethal state of combat between him and his enemy. And the casualty list was rapidly growing. Robert knew that he had to take drastic action against this monstrous criminal mastermind behind all this. Something-anything had to be done to stop him. Robert wanted to force him out of circulation. Because the war was now very real. This was certainly not over! It was surely just beginning. Robert became mad as hell that someone threatened his family-his parents this way. This unbelievable atrocity became too much to bear. Robert's emotions overcame him. He glanced at the horrendous sight of the three dead police officers and the dead 75 kg male orangutan lying on the floor with a knife inside its chest. He suddenly exploded in outrage at the awful visions his eyes were forced to witness as he cursed: "This dirty rotten son of a bitch responsible for this is going to pay. That low-down lunatic bastard is really going to get it. He thinks he can get away with this. With mass murder and playing these sick dirty games and insane tricks. No. No way!!! I swear to all of you – **I will kill him! I will kill this insane lunatic! He is finished when I get my hands on him!** He killed three of our men. He kills animals. He threatens people's families. He thinks he will frighten, scare and terrify us in order to stop the police from going after him and bringing him to justice for all his sick crimes! There is nothing he won't do. **Well – there isn't anything I won't do to eradicate him from all our lives once and for all!!! That is a promise! This bastard will not stop me from getting him!** Now, this is what I want done also," Robert said now glancing at his police officers swarming the premises of his parents' business. "I want you to contact every local zoo in the entire State of New York. I want you to question the entire zoo management hierarchy. From the zoo directors all the way down to all the zookeepers - and see if any of them has found a missing orangutan from their cages. And then contact me immediately. Once you establish which zoo this great ape was stolen from, then I want a team of cops sent down there, until you get me all the answers of the culprit or culprits responsible!"

The cops nodded their heads together.

Two hours later, Robert was notified of the answers he sought. The local Brooklyn Zoo Director reported a missing orangutan. Also, four overnight zookeepers were found dead before the cage of the missing orangutan. They were shot to death in the head and heart. Robert was also informed that the cage of the missing orangutan (now confirmed dead), was left open. And police ballistics investigators identified from the recovered bullets inside the four dead corpses, that the make and model of the gun used on the victims at the local zoo, possibly identically matched the same calibre of weapon used on the three dead police officers found at the Stewart family fish market business earlier. The bullets were exactly the same. That meant same killers. The police suspected more than one killer was responsible. Especially since it would take more than one man or person to kidnap an orangutan from a local zoo. Perhaps partners in crime, each armed with the same calibre weapon that fired the exact same bullets. But no other witnesses were found who saw anything at the zoo. The only available witnesses at the time of the orangutan's extraction from the zoo, were the zookeepers, but of course, they were all unfortunately killed!

Same killers meant same mastermind behind all the deaths! And Robert Stewart knew who that mastermind was. Robert Stewart prepared himself to move in for the enemy's kill before the enemy got him first!

Thirdly: The Archbishop of New York City & The President of the United States:

The next evening inside his station house office at approximately 9:00 p.m., Robert Stewart received an unexpected visit from a young brunette woman extremely eager to see him. Her very nervous and edgy demeanour marred a tad the otherwise natural attractiveness of this twenty-two-year-old appearing shaken lady named Susan Daley.

She went straight to the point as she seemed not only edgy but also scared as hell. Hence, she was desperate to spill the beans somewhat to this heroic cop as quickly as possible, in hopes that Robert may alleviate her desperately troubled mind.

As a worried young woman, she blurted out her words hurriedly. She was truly a desperate woman with an incredibly shocking story of woe and lamentation she had to report to the police. And she chose the most famous of them all 'Robert Stewart' to reveal her startling tale to.

She cried frantically in a determined tell-all frenzy: "My name is Susan Daley. I am part of the New York City Archbishop's team. I am in fact his Personal Assistant. I take care of prioritizing and planning his daily diary with briefings – and my duties also include the day-to-day management of his engagements. Now, please Commander Stewart, hear me out. I am here to report a murder that is about to take place. **Your murder!** And the Archbishop of this State and the United States President are in on the conspiracy to kill you. They are in cahoots together to smoke you out of your conscious state of always being on guard, so they can effectively lure you to a place to be killed! This is urgent. This warrants your immediate attention. Please. I am here to report this serious crime of conspiracy to commit murder by my boss and the country's leader. I am here out of desperation to save your life. I also plan to resign my duties immediately from the archbishop's team, as I refuse to get involved in his illegal schemes. I don't want him to drag me into his criminal activities. You see, Commander Stewart. I am scared. I am very scared. And I fear that if you don't protect me, the archbishop may also have me killed as he plans to kill you. And he may blackmail and threaten me to go along with his illegalities. And I am worried I may end up going to prison for the rest of my life if I associate with him any longer!

"You see, Commander. I got very suspicious of the archbishop when he kept complaining about you to me in private. He says that he hates you. He says that he wants revenge against you because he blames you for the deaths of certain priests in the past, during your investigation concerning the activities of specific corrupt operatives inside the Catholic Church. So, he keeps saying how he wants to destroy you before you ever have a chance to destroy him as well. And since he kept telling me those things in private inside his house where I usually worked for him, I feared that he would suck me into his web of deceit and ask me to go along with his plans of assisting to kill you. So, I became very frightened of this. And I decided to secretly record his conversations he had in private. I planted a tape recorder behind some books on a bookshelf inside his private office of his $30 million mansion in Manhattan - and I obtained evidence of a very incriminating conversation he had with the United States President this afternoon. Of course, you know the president flew to New York yesterday for some pretentious hypocritical concern he had in regards to the exposed corruption of two of this state's heads: The Governor and Lieutenant Governor who were exposed and dealt with accordingly by your hands. Now the true purpose of the State visit by the president of this country was to be invited privately inside the archbishop's personal home-his mansion in Manhattan to discuss the plan of your murder! In secret!

"Inside my purse, I have the tape with the incriminating conversation, the damning evidence you desperately need which took place between the Archbishop and the United States President, concerning you. Meaning, their diabolical plans to have you assassinated in such a way that their participation would never be suspected. And they would get away with it by maintaining a clean façade and clean hands to the public. I cannot believe it. The archbishop discussed plans of your murder whilst wearing his cassock robe and his large cross on a chain. It was frightening to me. I couldn't believe my eyes. I couldn't believe my ears. So that's why I came…to report this in order to save myself from his evil clutches and to save you as well, Commander Stewart!"

She quickly handed him the tape from her purse.

Robert Stewart immediately played the tape using his cassette player/recorder, listening to the incriminating conversation of the Archbishop and President's plans to have him killed.

This was what they were saying:

'Look at what Robert Stewart did to the Governor and Lieutenant Governor of this State!' said the president.

'Look at what he did to all those priests not so long ago who worked with me inside the Catholic Church!' hinted the archbishop.

'I know. His actions are hitting a little too close to home. He has to be dealt with quickly and drastically. I mean - how would it look for the White House if he even discredits this country's leader? Robert Stewart is crazy. He is insane. He is unpredictable. What or who is next on his shit list. Me? The United States President of this country. Nothing and no one are off-limits to him. He will damn us all to hell. I say we damn him first, what about you, Archbishop?'

The archbishop concurred: 'I agree with everything you are saying, Mr. President. Robert Stewart wouldn't think twice whenever he decides to attack us. So why should we fear burying him first? He is very dangerous to us. He is dangerous to the Church. He is dangerous to the White House. He is dangerous to everyone.'

The president wholeheartedly agreed. 'Yes. Too right. You are right indeed, Archbishop. We will fuck him before he ever turns us into fags behind bars. If Robert rids this city and country of Organised Crime as he intends, then that will drastically affect our incomes. We get rich by the very crooks we serve. There is no percentage in lifting up the poor. The poor are there to be trodden over by society. The rich are our benefactors. They pay us immensely for services we are able to deliver them, simply because we are smart enough to be in the right positions of demand at the right time. No matter how much we try to keep our hands clean publicly, with a man like Robert Stewart, we have no other recourse but to dirty our hands privately in any means necessary to rid his evil stench from our paths. If we do not dispose of him, well, you only need to look at what happened recently to the Governor and the Lieutenant Governor of this State. Because that will be us. That fate of death will be thrown at us next if we do not extract that menacing cop once and for all from the picture. TO RID HIM FROM OUR FUCKING LIVES. You and I have been friends for a long time. You married me and my wife five years ago when you were a simple priest. We attended each other's homes. We drank wine together. We ate dinner together. Robert Stewart now looms over us as a possible threat to our allegiance together. He threatens our eternal friendship. And now we must plan Robert Stewart's murder together!'

'True. Very true,' demanded the archbishop. 'You see, all our plots and plans are ordinarily very well-conceived plots and plans.'

'Yes, they are!' said the president, 'And they always would be if we live in a world without a psycho cop such as Robert Stewart in it, who's always waiting around the corner ready to expose our secrets and prosecute our crimes. And imprison us. You see, Archbishop; this really has little to do with Robert's role as either a homicide cop or a plainclothes police official serving inside the police department's detective division.'

'What do you mean?' asked the archbishop.

The president of the United States replied, 'Robert Stewart is a member of a very well-funded International Crime-Fighting Organisation. This international crime-fighting organisation covers every country in the world. The West, the East, The Middle East – everywhere! Now the participants of this organisation are really a secret. But let me tell you something. One man: one threat: one menace we know so happens to be a member of this organisation. His name is Robert Stewart. And just as he is regarded as the top cop in New York City - he is, at the same time, regarded as this international crime-fighting organisation's most dangerous agent. That bastard cop so happens to be also a very menacing international crime fighter. And that is a very sad story for us. This revelation of who he really is spells nothing but doom and gloom for US ALL! So, Archbishop - now you know how truly dangerous this man-this cop really is. Now you can bear witness to the true credentials of his not-so-well-known resume and his very secret background. A background I must add which also spells disaster for us both! Robert Stewart is not only a danger to us, but he is a true genius at solving cases. I mean, where a man like him is concerned, you just never know what he knows and what he suspects about any of us. We don't know when he could be watching us. We can never tell when he will be storming through our houses with a legion of police officials holding arrest warrants with our names attached to them. Many people in the past have underestimated him - and so many of them have either wound up in prison or dead or both!

'NOW, I have a plan to get rid of him for good whilst maintaining no complicity to our necessary actions we must take against him.'

'You mean, concerning his murder?' asked the archbishop.

The president clarified: 'Yes, exactly. A lot of my current campaigns for Republican presidential re-election next year are being funded and bankrolled by my sponsor, Dante Rolando. Dante Rolando is the man we will obtain the services for the task of killing Robert Stewart.

'Dante is also concerned about the threat Robert Stewart poses against him. This is how dangerous Robert is. This is the story Dante told me. Every time Robert catches a drug courier, such as a boat-keeper, he checks through the files in customs, to establish a pattern of conduct of these drugs and/or arms couriers. He checks the files at customs to see which checkpoints they use. And if they use the same checkpoint, thus establishing a pattern; and if he establishes this evidence whereby a drug and/or arms courier enters the same checkpoint, then that customs official gets on Robert's radar. So, Robert not only busts the drug couriers and their suppliers and dealers, but also puts the customs official under investigation for suspicion of accepting bribes - and he relentlessly pursues that individual and does not stop until he nails that person to the wall. And no matter how someone such as Dante tries to cover his tracks by killing all the witnesses around him - and destroying all the evidence – Robert Stewart still finds a way to finagle an ingenious infiltration scheme to extract that buried information through other mysterious means. So, that is why Dante Rolando considers Robert Stewart's existence a great big threat to him. He is too eager for the task in finally eliminating Robert Stewart. I spoke to him privately through intermediaries. And those go-betweens had sent back word to me that a hitman for the job has already been chosen. And the plan to get rid of Robert Stewart is already underway. We will use force to oust him out of the police department and his international crime-fighting unit. So, let us make a toast to us three forming the new Axis powers: me, you and Dante. And our united cooperative efforts which will see the demise of Robert Stewart. Because once Dante's stepson Marcus who volunteered to kill Robert for us, does indeed kill him, then you, me and Dante can form an eternal unholy alliance, filled with money and prosperity for us all in a world that no longer has Robert Stewart in it. So let us make a toast to the death of Robert Stewart. May he not rest in peace!'

Robert Stewart ejected the tape from the cassette player/recorder inside his office after he finished listening to all its contents.

What was the verdict?

The incriminating evidence of the four identified evil and immoral villains on that tape which included the archbishop of this state, the president of this country and Dante Rolando and his stepson Marcus was damning indeed.

Robert had solid concrete evidence on recorded tape spoken inside the archbishop's own personal house mansion in Manhattan, that the archbishop, the president, Dante Rolando and his stepson Marcus, were all united in the plan of his-Robert Stewart's murder.

This evidence was ground-breaking. It was bloody well earth-shattering. It was fantastic. It was frigging amazing!

The evidence on that tape was enough for the police to issue official arrest warrants against the archbishop of New York, the president of the United States, Dante Rolando and the hitman stepson Marcus.

Robert stared at this young woman Susan Daley who got him this evidence with meek grateful eyes. He smiled warmly to her. His eyes were filled with many thanks for her courage, decency and good-natured spirit, to approach him with this tape which incriminated some of the most deadly and dangerous criminals in this country. Robert was suddenly overjoyed. He finally got the goods on Dante Rolando and a few deserving others.

Robert immediately alerted his cavalry of the breakthrough via this incriminating tape, he forwarded to them as solid police evidence, which would even immediately result in the US President's removal from office on the basis of criminal activity, resulting in impeachment and consecutive conviction for his part in committing high crimes, which was exactly what he would be charged with. That would result in indicting and prosecuting a sitting president.

But just as Robert's army of police colleagues prepared for the arrest of the four major criminal figures (as the four accused co-conspiring villains were all plunged together in this state of New York), Susan Daley was still shaking inside Robert's office. She was crying and still preoccupied with dreadful thoughts that the archbishop could have enlisted her involvement in such heinous crimes, which would have resulted in her sharing the same fate as her former boss faced: life imprisonment.

All along she was worried about being involved in her ex-boss's devious schemes and murderous plans. Her mind could not shake off the eeriness of what she had experienced. And that was part of the reason she approached Robert. And another part was to see justice served. She was also scared for her life and feared that her ex-boss may try to kill her the same way he conspired to kill Robert. And she had no hesitation voicing such concerns to him.

Robert embraced her gently and comforted her by insisting: "He won't. He won't hurt you! None of them will get to you. You're safe. They're all going to prison for a very long time. In fact, the incriminating tape would be enough corroborating evidence to have them all locked up in prison for the rest of their lives. So please don't worry about anything, Susan, ok. They will never be able to get close to you, I promise you that!"

But Robert Stewart shortly received some bad news on two fronts. Two of the arrests were successful, but two of them were nowhere to be found when the police raided the Rolando household in the city, tearing it apart.

Dante Rolando and his stepson Marcus were nowhere to be found. They somehow escaped police apprehension. They vanished. Gone from the premises. They disappeared without a trace.

Dante Rolando disappeared seemingly in thin air, leaving no clue behind as to his current whereabouts. And he vanished, taking his stepson with him. They were both hidden somewhere nowhere to be seen or heard from. And the police failed to locate them thus far.

The police psychiatrists situated in many police precincts across the city began doing profiles on all mass murdering tyrants, all the way back to Adolf Hitler, in hopes to get a direct line on their most wanted man – and obtain a complete insight against their target suspected, Domenico Armando, currently on the run from the authorities, as a gigantic police manhunt tore loose across all the streets of New York City, combing the entire vicinity, out looking for him.

This was a desperate search. A desperate struggle to catch both Dante Rolando and his killer stepson.

Every moment they were unapprehended spelled trouble, big trouble for everyone.

Robert Stewart and John McCallum joined the police search parties on the streets of New York City hunting down their enemy.

Robert memorised all of their target's files and locations of old buildings he could be using to hide inside, since the days he was (allegedly) known as Domenico Armando.

Robert drove through the streets inside his unmarked car with his police partner in hot pursuit of their target - and searched what seemed abandoned warehouses, office buildings and previous houses belonging to Domenico Armando.

Robert and John were on a crucial campaign to get their man, no matter what. They would work both day and night, whatever it took to find him and make him pay for all the deaths and misery he had caused in his chaotically destructive life thus far; and the further lives he planned to ruin if they did not catch him quickly.

Robert hinted: "We have to get this bastard Dante Rolando. We have to find this crazy lunatic Domenico Armando and his deranged stepson Marcus out on the loose, on the run with him. We have to get this maniac Armando. We cannot let him get away from us for another moment!"

John McCallum agreed. He witnessed the almost manic desperation in Robert's eyes. John understood all too well. He felt the same way as he exclaimed: "And we will get him! We will get them both, don't you worry! The two of them are not going to get away! They are both out there somewhere hiding in this city, but they won't get far! We'll catch them before they victimise somebody else. We'll nail them both before they have a chance to kill another life! They are not going to get away this time.

"We have police patrols combing the streets of this entire city. We have set up roadblocks at every exit of this city. We have the private and commercial airstrip terminals watched. We have the train stations and bus depots under surveillance. Now he is still somewhere here in New York hiding inside one of the five boroughs.

"He is either here in Brooklyn or one of the other four boroughs. But he is not going to escape us for long. We're going to force him into our hands. Our police patrols are searching every car leaving this city. No vehicle - light, medium or heavy will remain unsearched by our armies of police troops blanketing the streets of this city. That's an order!

"Dante thinks he can hide from us forever, but he can't. He is not invisible. And we're going to get him!"

Robert Stewart immediately received a call on his cellular mobile phone. It was not a private number. The number was intentionally revealed to him. Robert recognised the phone number. It was his enemy, Dante Rolando.

Robert first hinted to his police partner seated in the front passenger seat aside him the identity of the caller before he answered his phone and said, "Robert Stewart!"

The caller on the other side of the phone first chuckled in laughter and then said firmly into his end of the call: "This is Dante Rolando."

Robert interrupted him and shouted angrily, "You mean Domenico Armando!"

His enemy chuckled this time approvingly and said: "How is the search party going, my old friend Robert Stewart?"

Robert replied, "You're not going to get away Armando or Rolando, whichever name you choose to call yourself these days!"

"Really?" Domenico snapped. "This time I will not end up in prison ever. This time I will come out on top. I will win Robert Stewart. You hear me? I will win this game between us!"

Robert snapped, "It's not a game Armando!"

Dante Rolando also known as Domenico Armando insisted, "We shall see, won't we. I gave you the archbishop and the country's president out of sheer spite and hatred for them both. Yes. We did business together, but I wanted to destroy the two of them, especially this country's president, because he kept this country so wickedly corrupt and morally bankrupt, that it cost me the life of my beautiful stepdaughter Maria. So, you understand my motives. Anyhow, I am going to disappear from circulation forever, Robert Stewart. You or your police friends will never find me. And when I disappear for good, no one will ever know when or if I will resurface again!"

Both ends clicked.

In the conclusive finale concerning this battle of the long bitter war between Robert Stewart and his arch-enemy nemesis Domenico Armando, the result this time was a terrible stalemate!